SISTERS OF CRESCENT VALLEY
Forget the Former Things

CLAUDIA EGGERT HARRIER

WESTBOW
PRESS®
A DIVISION OF THOMAS NELSON
& ZONDERVAN

WestBow Press books may be ordered through booksellers or by contacting:

WestBow Press
A Division of Thomas Nelson & Zondervan
1663 Liberty Drive
Bloomington, IN 47403
www.westbowpress.com
844-714-3454

ISBN: 978-1-6642-8663-4 (sc)
ISBN: 978-1-6642-8664-1 (hc)
ISBN: 978-1-6642-8665-8 (e)

Library of Congress Control Number: 2022922898

Print information available on the last page.

WestBow Press rev. date: 12/28/2022

To Jesus Christ,
who holds me close and walks me through the challenges of life,
and to my husband, Stephen,
who cheers me on and supports me with his love.
Forget the former things;
Do not dwell on the past.
See, I am doing a new thing!
Now it springs up;
Do you not perceive it?
I am making a way in the wilderness
and streams in the wasteland.
—Isaiah 43:18–19 (NIV)

Chapter 1

Something didn't seem quite right as Jodie blinked the day into view. "What time is it anyway?" A few more blinks and a glance out the window partially answered her puzzle. Clouds hung low, and the sun had apparently crept below the horizon. The clock said 6:30, but was it 6:30 a.m. and the day was just dawning, or was it 6:30 p.m. and the day was ending? She wasn't sure. Her brain seemed to be full of cotton balls. She shook her head a few times to clear it.

More than just about anything, Jodie hated being sick. Yesterday morning—at least she thought it was yesterday morning—she had called in sick. That medicine she had taken had really knocked her out, and she had slept so soundly. She let her legs hang over the side of the bed as she bent back to stretch and raise her arms to get the kinks out. At least she didn't ache like she did when she went to sleep yesterday—or was it today?

As she descended the stairs, she could hear the television in the family room. Jason hadn't left for work yet. She breathed deeply. Yes, he had made some coffee. She could use a jolt to jump-start her brain.

"Well, well! Hello, Sleeping Beauty!" He winked at her. "It's nice to see you have returned to the land of the living."

Jodie briefly noted the commercial that was playing and then turned her attention to Jason. Not veiling her confusion, she asked, "What day is it? Is it morning or evening?"

"Wow! You really did just rejoin the land of the living, didn't you? You remind me of Ebenezer Scrooge when he didn't know what day it was after the visits from the spirits on Christmas Eve."

"Well?" Jodie pursed her lips and gave her husband a warning look.

"It's Tuesday, my sweets. Tuesday evening—and the current time is six forty-two. Are you okay?"

"Yeah, I think I am. Whew! Tuesday evening." Shaking her head again, she continued, "I feel so much better than I did this morning, but my head is still pretty groggy."

"Here, come sit down, and let me get you something to eat."

How in the world did she ever get a husband like Jason? He was so naturally thoughtful and helpful. Jodie thought back over the last five years since they were married. They had been married long enough to know that every day was not perfect but also long enough to understand that their marriage relationship was far more important than the petty arguments in which they sometimes engaged. Her cheeks reddened as she remembered how she recently had gotten on Jason's case for forgetting to pick up bread on his way home from work. How had that trite offense grown into a full-blown argument? How could she accuse him of not caring for her simply because she had intended to have ham sandwiches for dinner and needed the bread? To think that she had dissolved in tears over such a little thing! Now, here he was fixing her dinner. She looked at Jason with admiration. "I was about to shower and get ready for work. I guess it was a good thing I came down here first."

Jason stirred the soup in the pot. "Even if it was morning, I don't think you should be going to work. You need to give yourself a little more time to really recuperate."

"I know I should, but they are so shorthanded. Believe me, I know what it is like to work short."

"Yes, but you don't want to go back when you aren't sure you are truly over whatever you had. You don't want to spread it to the others or to your patients."

"Who do you think I got it from? I work with sick people every day. I am bound to catch a few of the bugs they bring in. I would just think of it as *giving back*!" Jodie flashed a smile. "I know. You are right. I really should go ahead and call in tonight so they can get an on-call for tomorrow. Then I should be fully ready to go back on Thursday."

"Sounds like a plan. Take tomorrow and make sure you are recovered. You've been working some long hours, and after a while, it begins to take a toll on your body."

"You sound like a doctor. So what do you prescribe, Doctor Jason?" Jodie rose from the couch and made her way next to her husband at the stove.

"Drink plenty of fluids. Get lots of rest. Take two aspirin and call me in the morning."

Jodie squeezed him around the waist. "You always know how to make me laugh."

"My specialty and my pleasure!" Jason returned the squeeze and wrapped her in a full embrace. "And now, my patient, your dinner is served. For your dining pleasure tonight, we have some delectable chicken noodle soup, the ultimate in saltine crackers, crisp celery sticks, and a tall glass of Florida's best orange juice. You know you need that extra vitamin C when you are sick."

"Yes, Doctor!" Jodie took her place at the table, and Jason sat across from her. "Aren't you having anything?"

"I had a huge sandwich and potato chips earlier. I'm still feeling full. I'll settle for tea and some delightful conversation."

"Well, that's quite sweet of you, Doctor."

"I'm not a real doctor. I just play one when my wife is sick!" Jason reached across the table and took her hands in his. They both bowed their heads as Jason thanked God for the food and prayed that soon Jodie would be completely well.

"So how was your day at work? What did you guys get done today?" Jodie asked.

"I've had better days. First, the pavers for the project were four hours late, and some of my guys do not switch gears very easily. I had to really stay on them to get them working on the landscaping on the east side of the drive. Excuse me—I think I will get that tea. Would you like one?" Jason made his way to their new single-cup brewer.

"No, I'm good with my orange juice," replied Jodie as she raised her glass as if making a toast. "It is really going to be stunning when you finish that project. I can't wait to see it. What do the homeowners think of what's been done so far?"

"Well, the wife, Jillian, is fine with it all. She seems to love every new thing. Her husband, Mark, is a whole different story. He has been watching way too many backyard makeover shows, where they have a whole production company working behind the scenes, a bevy of friends and neighbors who show up to do all the grunt work, and the project is completed in fifty minutes or less."

Snapping a saltine, Jodie asked, "So did you get the driveway done?"

"Oh, no." He shook his head. "It will take us at least another two full days—that's one monster drive. But you can already start to see how awesome it will be when it is done." He set his tea on the table.

"You have been so gifted in creative design! Promise me that you will take me to see it as soon as it is done!"

Taking her hand to his lips and giving it a gentle kiss, he smiled. "I always do, my love. Whenever I finish something, I am so excited to have my silent partner come and see it."

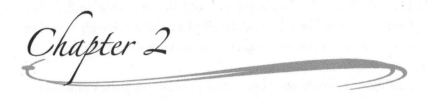

Chapter 2

The next morning, Jodie got up with Jason and made coffee. As she packed his lunch, she thought about what she might do that day. Oh, she knew she had to rest, but there was a side of her that felt like she was getting a free day off and that she needed to make the most of it. Maybe she could clean out the hall closet—no, that would be too much work. She needed to do something fun.

Since the weather had not yet completely turned to the fall gray and the temperature was supposed to get up to near seventy degrees, maybe she could plan to do something outside. That was it! She would clean up the deck and then spend some time lounging there with her Kindle and a tall glass of iced green tea. She brightened at the thought of a few hours with nothing to do, nothing but to pamper herself a bit. She might even make a special dinner for Jason. Yes, it would be stuffed pork chops with her rustic mashed potatoes—two of his favorites.

Jason snatched his lunch, gave Jodie a quick kiss, and headed off to work. On days like this, he liked to get the crew started by seven o'clock and then work a ten-hour day, plus one hour for lunch and breaks. Hopefully, today would be a better day, and the guys would be careful to not make any more errors in the paver pattern. He eagerly drove to the project site. It was wonderful to be able to work doing what he loved to do. He could easily picture himself doing this for the rest of his life.

Jodie showered and pulled on her favorite everyday jeans. This was starting out as a very good day. A quick dash to the grocery store yielded thick-cut pork chops and fresh kale that she needed to make dinner. Now she was out to tackle the deck. Who would have thought that so much could accumulate on a deck during just one summer? There was that plastic chair that had broken when she stood on it to water her hanging basket. She set that chair next to the trash can. Tomorrow it would be taken away. Grabbing a cloth and a bowl of soapy water, she started scrubbing the table and chairs. "So much grime—so little time." She smiled. She placed a tablecloth on the table and designed a centerpiece with a bowl of fresh-cut mums and a few jar candles. A quick sweeping of the deck, and her job was done.

There. Now she could get on to her tea and reading. Jodie unfolded the lounge chair and set the little plastic deck table next to it. Assuring herself that she was resting to do her body good served to assuage her slightly guilty heart. She truly was not being lazy; she was recovering. The next several hours allotted her time to complete the book she had started last week and to begin a new one.

Life is good, she thought, and she leaned back and shut her eyes. If only she and Jason had a baby, everything would be absolutely perfect.

The couple had been trying for a pregnancy for over a year and had not been successful. Some preliminary tests had not revealed any specific reason for her not to be able to get pregnant. Each month, her discouragement grew. She tried so hard to hand this over to God, but it seemed that she could not accept that it might be God's will that she and Jason would never have a child of their own.

A call from Jason let her know that he was planning on being home around seven thirty. Jodie couldn't wait to see his face when he saw the dinner she had made. She would serve it by candlelight on her freshly cleaned deck. She chopped apples, kale, and goat cheese to make a salad that she had recently discovered online. At 7:20, she finished setting the deck table, including lighting the candles in jars, a gift from a friend. A peek inside the oven assured her that the stuffed pork chops were near perfection and would finish at just the right time. She mashed the potatoes and stirred in a bit of cheese, sour cream, and fresh-cut chives to give them that loaded baked potato flavor that Jason loved. She put some broccoli into the vegetable steamer so that she could quickly finish it when everything else was ready. She wanted it to be perfectly bright green and tender crisp when she brought it to the table.

Jason still had not appeared at 7:45, and Jodie was concerned that her pork chops would get dry. By eight o'clock, she was getting a wee bit miffed. "Why in the world did he say seven thirty if he really meant around eight—or later?"

At 8:15, Jodie called Jason's phone. There was no answer. Sometimes he forgot to take his charger, and his phone would be dead by the end of the day. "Why couldn't he be more responsible?" Amid her stewing, her phone rang. She recognized the number that was displayed. Probably the hospital was calling to see if she was going to be at work tomorrow.

In response to her "Hello," the woman on the other end asked, "Is this Jodie Igland?"

"Yes, this is she."

"Jodie, this is Margaret Shuman from Crescent Valley Memorial Medical Center. I am sorry to tell you that your husband, Jason, was in an auto accident, and he is here in our emergency department." The voice on the phone sounded so professional.

"Is he okay?" Panic bit at Jodie's voice.

"I do not have many details for you currently, but he is conscious. His doctor said to prepare you by telling you that he suffered quite a few serious injuries."

"I will be right there. Can you let him know that I am on my way?" Jodie's voice broke as she tried to wrap her brain around what was being relayed to her.

"Yes, I will be glad to do that. When you get here, please stop by the registration desk and fill out the admission forms. Oh, and be sure to bring your insurance card."

"Okay. I should be there in about fifteen minutes."

Chapter 3

Jodie's brain, which had been so fuzzy yesterday, was now cranked up to a frenzy. She ran to the kitchen and turned off the oven and stove. She should have put all the food away, but she didn't want to take any more time. Grabbing her purse, she dashed out of the house and drove to the hospital. She made that trip every day she worked, but this time, everything seemed foreign. Jason, her Jason, was in an emergency room right now. She didn't know the extent of his injuries, but the patient services coordinator had said they were serious. Her training and experience as a nurse had not prepared her for this when it came to someone so close to her. Tears trickled out of the corners of her eyes as she prayed, "Oh, dear Father, please take care of Jason. Help the staff to figure out what is wrong and what needs to be done for him. Please, God, don't let him die." Jodie could not believe that the possibility of Jason's death had even crept into her brain, but it had, and there it was.

It felt so weird to park in the emergency department parking instead of the remote employee lot. She fairly flew into the hospital and scurried up to the desk.

"Hi. I'm Jodie Igland, and my husband, Jason, was brought in by ambulance." She was breathless—not so much because she had rushed to get there but because of the stress of the situation.

"Jodie, it's me—Kayla!" The woman behind the partition looked up with concern.

"I'm sorry, Kayla." Jodie ran her fingers through her hair. "I guess I am in such a state that I didn't even look to see who you were."

"Here, let me take you to see Jason for a few minutes, and then you can come back to do the paperwork."

"Thanks, Kayla." Jodie's reply was barely above a whisper.

Kayla handed her a name tag that allowed access to Jason's room. Pointing to the door to her left, she continued, "He is in room T-3. Do you want me to take you there?"

"No, I know the way," Jodie responded, having picked up on the "T-3"—Trauma 3. She knew that T-3 was the room reserved in the ER for the most severe trauma patients.

Before she even reached the room, Jodie could hear Dr. Parker calling out instructions to those around. "Let's get a CAT scan of the brain and an abdominal ultrasound stat. Also, get the orthopedic surgeon on-call stat and an anesthesiologist. Do we have any of the pre-op bloodwork back yet? And where are we on those four units of red cells? He has lost quite a bit already. Reserve an operating room and get a scrub team to be ready to go in thirty minutes."

Jodie stepped inside the beehive of activity and made her way to Jason. He had a deep laceration on his forehead, and his light brown hair was matted. His whole upper body was exposed as the doctor checked out every part of his body. Her husband's eyes were pinched closed, his teeth clenched, and his jaw set tight—all signs that Jodie recognized as responses to the pain.

"Jason?" She touched his cheek.

His eyes opened with a scared little boy look.

Jodie bent over and kissed his lips. "Oh, sweetheart! I love you!"

Jason nodded slightly and whisper-grunted back, "I love you too. I can't believe this happened."

"Don't worry about that. You're going to be okay. I know you will get the very best care here."

Dr. Parker turned to Jodie. "We're taking Jason to get some studies done to check for internal injuries. We'll let you know as soon as we get some answers. We know for sure that he has two broken legs and probably a fractured pelvis. We have him scheduled for surgery as soon as our surgeon gets here. It will be sometime within the next hour."

The first unit of blood cells arrived and was quickly hung. With that, the team wheeled Jason out of the room and headed for radiology. Jodie, still stunned, made her way back to the reception desk to complete the dreaded paperwork. Why did paperwork always have to take people away from where they really wanted and needed to be? And right now, she wanted to be with Jason. Hopefully, she could finish the forms quickly and get back to him.

Even though the paperwork was on the computer and Jodie only had to answer Kayla's questions, it seemed to take forever. Her insurance card was confirmed and scanned into the system, and then she was free to go find Jason. She took the elevator to the fourth floor and radiology. She was glad that at least she knew her way around the building. She was told that Jason would be done there in about ten to fifteen minutes, so she settled into the waiting room. She glanced at the magazines on the table. Crescent Valley Memorial had a "Comfort Improvement Project" recently that included outlawing old magazines, so each department had subscriptions to four magazines, and the staff was to keep only the current editions in their waiting areas. It looked like radiology was doing well with that task—all the magazines were current, and today's paper was on the side table. Jodie picked up the paper and stared at the front page. Nothing seemed to register. All she could do was think about Jason and his injuries.

She looked up when she heard her name. Kaiden from radiology was wheeling Jason out. "Jodie, they told me you were waiting here. We are going straight to surgery. You can come along with us, and the surgeon will fill you in on what's what."

Jodie hustled to Jason's side and took his right hand. The life-giving cells were flowing into his left arm, and an added IV had been started in his left hand. Jodie knew that the red on his face and body wasn't going to hurt him—it was just evidence of the hurt that had already been done. When they reached the pre-op holding area, a nurse met them.

"Hi! I'm Shelly. I'm going to clean you up a bit to lessen the risk of infection during surgery. I will be as gentle as possible because I know you are in a lot of pain."

With that, Shelly opened a pre-op kit and began cleaning Jason's face. Only after his face had been scrubbed clean did Jodie notice how pale Jason was. He appeared to have lost much blood already, and now he was going into surgery, where he would lose some more. Shelly moved down to Jason's chest and arms, scrubbing them with the antibacterial soap.

When Shelly removed the sheet from Jason's legs, Jodie gasped. His legs were bent at odd angles. She hadn't seen that in the ER. There was a large wound on his left thigh. Shelly gingerly cleansed the cut by flooding it with a disinfectant and scrubbing all the skin around it. Both legs were swamped with the soap and then painted with the antiseptic. Lastly, she uncovered his pelvic area and cleaned there. She shaved the outside of his left hip and stated, "I am shaving the rest of the area just to minimize any infection. We will insert a catheter once we are in the surgery suite." Having completed Jason's bath and shave, Shelly picked up her supplies and left the room.

Jodie gave Jason a weak smile. "You clean up nicely, cowboy." Jason squeezed her hand in reply.

Shelly returned with a filled syringe. She scanned Jason's wristband and the barcode on the syringe. "This will help you to feel better. It is a pain killer that will relax you before the surgery. You may feel a little tingle as it flows into your arm." Shelly inserted the needle into the IV tube. Jason welcomed the tingle, as he knew it signaled that relief was on its way.

The second unit of red cells arrived, and after two nurses went through the validation protocol, it was hung in place of the empty first unit. As the life-sustaining cells flowed into his arm, Jason took a deep breath—the first sign that his body was beginning to relax.

"You should start to feel more comfortable in just a few minutes." Shelly checked Jason's blood pressure and pulse. "Your vitals will be monitored automatically by the cuff and the patches that we put on your chest. I am also attaching this little probe to your finger to monitor your oxygen saturation."

As Shelly left, Dr. Hernandez, the orthopedic surgeon, entered and introduced himself. "Well, Jason, I have good news, and I have bad news. The good news—no, I'd say, great news—is that none of your injuries appear to be life-threatening, and you can expect to have an almost full recovery from all of them. Also, there does not appear to be any internal organ damage or bleeding. The bad news is that your legs are both broken—your left femur, in fact, is quite shattered—and you do, indeed, have a broken pelvis. The left side has two fractures."

"So, Doctor, what exactly will you be doing in surgery besides setting the bones in my legs? And what do you do for a broken pelvis?" Jason asked.

"This is not an easy surgery, and each one is unique. I will be using screws, pins, and plates to stabilize the pelvis. Some will be internal, but there will also be an external frame. The external frame will stay in place for several months. I will be putting a titanium rod down your left femur, and we will see what bone pieces I will need to remove." Dr. Hernandez drew in a long breath as he turned toward Jason. "Right now, we need to get you to surgery and start the repairs. You ready?"

Jason momentarily shut his eyes and nodded.

"Okay then. I'll see you in the OR in a few minutes." With that, the surgeon headed out to scrub in preparation for the task before him.

Jodie fought back tears as she struggled to maintain her composure. "Oh, Jason!" she whispered. "You mean so much to me! My precious, precious Jason!" She squeezed his hand again and pressed her lips against his. As hard as she tried to keep them in, she couldn't keep a few tears from spilling onto his face.

The pain medication was causing Jason to become drowsy. "I love you, Jodie. God is going to bring us through this."

"I know He will," she whispered back. She placed her hands on both sides of his face and kissed his lips once more before Shelly and an orderly wheeled Jason out of the room.

Chapter 4

It wasn't until the gurney turned the corner and Jason was whisked out of her sight that Jodie realized that she hadn't even contacted her parents yet—or Jason's parents either, for that matter. She suddenly felt very vulnerable and in need of her parents. Picking up her phone, she selected her dad's number. As soon as her dad answered, the dam breached, and tears streamed down her cheeks. "Daddy," she sobbed, "Jason was in a bad accident and is on his way to surgery."

Her dad did his best to comfort her as she told him all that she knew. "Honey, we'll be right there," he assured her. "We're on our way out the door right now."

After the call, Jodie felt that she could now handle notifying Jason's parents. They said that they would catch a flight out in the morning. She still had some time before her parents would arrive, so she called her sister, Kristen. The two had been so close growing up, but in recent years, they had seemed to have less and less in common. Their conversations often resulted in confrontations and conflict. This call, however, went well, and Kristen was very sympathetic to Jodie's plight.

Jodie rested her head against the back of the chair and silently prayed again for the surgeon, for the surgery, and for Jason's recovery. Her parents soon popped in the door, and Jodie ran into her mother's arms. "He's in surgery now," she sputtered.

"What are they doing?" her dad asked.

"He has some pretty bad lacerations, and both legs are broken—both his tibia and fibula on the right"—Jodie pointed toward her calf—"and the femur on the left." She moved her hand to her own left thigh.

13

"That sounds really bad," Dale responded as he wrapped his arms around his daughter.

"Yeah, it is! The worst injuries are his pelvis and left femur. His pelvis is broken in two places, and Dr. Hernandez—he's the orthopedic surgeon—said that his femur was shattered. Jason will have both internal and external hardware to put everything back together—screws, rods, and pins inside and screws to a bar outside." Jodie surprised herself that some of her nurse demeanor returned as she explained the technical part of Jason's injuries and the surgery.

"We can only give thanks that his life was spared and that he will recover." Bonnie hugged her daughter, and the three of them made their way to a group of chairs.

"There's more." Jodie drew in a deep breath. "The doctor says that because of the breaks and deep lacerations in his left femur, he may have also severed some nerves, and he may end up with limited movement of that leg."

"Oh, Jodie, I'm so sorry." Her dad reached out his hand to comfort her. "Let's pray for Jason right now."

The three held hands as Dale prayed for Jason's surgery and for grace for whatever lay before them. Upon his "Amen," he said, "I'm going to call Kristen and our pastor. Who else do we need to call right now?"

"I already called Kristen, and she was actually very kind to me, but we need to call Jason's crew and let them know they will need to work on their own tomorrow."

"What are they working on?" Dale asked.

"Right now, they are laying pavers on a driveway up in the Laurel Ridge area—some lawyer's house on the golf course. Jason would have all that information and his crew's phone numbers on his cell. Let me think—there's Matt Dawson, Rich Sanders, Phillip Northrup, Dave ..." Jodie ran her hand across her forehead. "Oh, what's his last name? He just started about a month ago. Dave Pressington or something like that. I think Jason would want Matt to be the crew leader right now."

"I'll take care of it," Dale responded.

"His phone would have been in his jeans pocket or in his truck." Jodie placed her head in her hands. "By the time I got here, they had already cut his jeans off him. I didn't think to ask for his stuff."

Dale patted his daughter's arm. "You sit tight. I will go and gather that stuff and make the phone calls."

"It would be in the emergency room, Dad. They should have a bag with all of Jason's belongings. Hopefully, they will let you have it. If they don't, call me, and I will give them the okay."

With that, Dale left the surgery waiting area. He was able to retrieve Jason's bag and found his cell phone in his jeans pocket as Jodie had said. He called Pastor Ron and asked him to put Jason on the prayer chain." It was funny that the name, prayer chain, still remained from the days when each person who received a call was to call the next on the chain with an urgent prayer request. Now everything was sent by email blast, and the serious things were usually on Facebook within ten minutes or less.

Jodie was shocked to see her sister walk through the door. Kristen hurried to Jodie and hugged her.

Jodie said, "I didn't expect you to come. Are you off work?"

"Pete let me leave when I told him about the accident. He said that he could handle the rest of the cleanup since the coffee shop was closing soon."

"I'm glad you came." Bonnie stood and hugged her older daughter.

Kristen's recent relationship with her family had been very strained. She had dropped out of college and moved to New York to pursue a career in modeling or fashion design. She ended up working in a large fabric store in the fashion district, but she was never able to break into the fashion industry as either a designer or a model. While there, she had several romantic encounters and relationships. Like her career dreams, each of them looked promising, but each evaporated into nothingness. Depressed and financially broke, Kristen had returned to Crescent Valley to start over.

"I'm not entirely evil. I still have a heart," replied Kristen.

"I know you do, dear." Bonnie gave her oldest daughter another hug and kissed her lightly on her forehead.

Turning to her sister, Kristen asked, "Is there anything you need to have done or anything I can get for you?"

"Yes, now that you asked. I left dinner on the stove. There are stuffed pork chops that I just pulled out of the oven and left there, along with mashed potatoes. If you wouldn't mind stopping by my house and taking them home with you. Someone needs to eat it. And there are dishes on the deck table—and, oh my!" Jodie gasped and rubbed her face with both hands. "The candles—I left them burning. They are in jars, but would you take care of that?"

"I can do all of that," her sister replied. "But what do you need? I assume you will probably be spending the night here?"

"Yes, definitely," Jodie responded. "I will need some underwear and a change of clothes, my deodorant, toothbrush and toothpaste, and a hairbrush."

"Sure, I'm on it. After I get the food home, I'll be back." With that, Kristen took the offered keys, hugged her sister, and left the waiting room.

No sooner had Kristen left than Pastor Ron and his wife, Sylvia, entered the room. They both embraced Jodie.

"We came as soon as we could. How is Jason?" Pastor Ron asked.

"He is expected to be in surgery for several hours. His injuries were quite extensive, but none is believed to be life-threatening. The most severe damage was done to his broken pelvis and femur—they will take the longest time to repair," Jodie responded. "The surgeon said he will have lots of hardware installed."

Pastor Ron gathered the small group and prayed for Jason. The ensuing hours passed slowly for the family as they awaited word of the completion of the surgery.

A nurse Jodie did not recognize came to talk with the family. "Dr. Hernandez asked that I give you a brief update on his progress. He has completed the pelvic repair and has repaired the broken bones in both legs. He did find that some nerves and tendons had been severed in Jason's left thigh, and he called in a neurosurgeon to take care of those, as well as a plastic surgeon to stitch up the laceration on his forehead, so there should not be much of a scar there. Dr. Hernandez expects that they will all be done in about another twenty to thirty minutes. He, himself, will come out to talk more with you then. Jason is doing fine right now."

Chapter 5

Jodie and her parents breathed a collective sigh of relief to hear that the end of the surgery was in sight. They were surprised when Matt walked in. He was still in his work clothes and was sporting his Igland Landscaping cap. Jason had invested in caps for the crew instead of shirts, knowing that shirts would soon become grimy and stained, and the guys often went shirtless during much of the summer. Jodie thanked him for coming and filled him in on Jason's condition. Matt related that he had stopped by the body shop where Jason's pickup had been taken. "The pickup is totaled, I'm sure. Jason is lucky that he survived it. His guardian angel sure did double duty today."

"I know that God protected him. Do you know how it happened? "Jodie asked.

"The guy at the body shop said that an SUV ran the stop sign at Forty-Third and Tycoon Lane. It appeared that Jason swerved to the right to avoid him, but the SUV swerved that way also and smashed right into the driver's side and front end. I told them I would be back tomorrow to collect Jason's tools and ladders from the back. They assured me they would be secure overnight."

Jodie was so grateful that Matt had taken the initiative to check on the truck and get the tools out. "I really appreciate your doing all of that, Matt. I know Jason will be glad."

"I'm hoping that I can keep the crew working at the same pace so we can get that driveway done on schedule."

"I will speak for Jason here—you tell them that they are to give you the same cooperation and respect that they give Jason, or they will be without a job. Jason is going to be out for several months, at the very least, and he will be counting on all of you to continue with the projects he already has lined up." Jodie smiled at Matt, but her eyes conveyed firmness. Even though their own insurance and the other driver's insurance should cover their medical expenses and the truck, they would need the landscaping income to meet their other obligations.

Matt reached out his hand to Jodie. "You can count on me—and the crew. We will all work hard for Jason. I will make sure of that."

Jodie shook his hand and replied, "Thanks, Matt! Jason feels that he has a really good crew right now, but they just need direction and someone to call the shots for them."

Matt turned to leave. "Don't you worry about anything! Tell Jason not to worry either. I will stop back and see him after work on Friday—we should have the pavers all done by then. If he needs to tell us anything, feel free to call my cell. Make sure he knows that we've got this."

"Thanks again, Matt." Jodie smiled as Matt exited. She turned her attention back to her parents, Pastor Ron, and Sylvia. "I don't know what I would do without Matt taking over the crew."

"He seems like he is up to the job," Dale remarked. "I sure hope he can deliver. It will mean a great deal to Jason and take that stress out of his recovery."

A brief time later, Dr. Hernandez, wearing his scrubs and surgery cap, and with his mask pulled down around his neck, approached the family group. "Well, we're done, and Jason did exceptionally well. He is young, healthy, and strong. We have replaced three units of red cells, and the fourth is hanging. His body will soon make up for the rest. Like I told you prior to the surgery, Jodie, Jason is now the owner of quite a bit of shiny hardware. His pelvis has sixteen internal pins, four external screws, and a large plate. I also had to use an internal plate to secure the left femur. I reattached a couple of tendons there, and the neurosurgeon reattached some nerves. We'll just have to wait and see how much permanent damage he will have."

"What kind of permanent damage are we talking about?" Jodie asked. "I know Jason will want all the details as soon as he is alert."

"Well, that is rather difficult to predict at this time, but it is possible that he may suffer some permanent numbness and immobility in the left leg and foot, and he might have some difficulty in walking." Dr. Hernandez pursed his lips as he continued. "Right now, let's just hope for the best."

"We've been praying for that already," Jodie responded as she wiped a remaining tear from her eye. "That is, we and a whole group of people from our church and around the world—thanks to Facebook and other social media."

"I'm sure that can't hurt. I've seen people come through some pretty incredible things, and they attributed it to prayer. I'll stop in tomorrow morning and check on Jason. He should have a fairly good night—he will still have a lot of anesthesia on board. He will be on IV narcotics for the next several days, and then we will move him onto orals." The doctor shook hands with each of them and said to Jodie, "I will see you in the morning."

Two hours later, Jason was transferred to the orthopedic unit, and Jodie got herself situated for the night. Kristen had brought her the things that she had requested. She had also thought to bring some shampoo, cream rinse, a T-shirt, socks, and a clean pair of jeans. Jason woke up briefly and acknowledged Jodie's presence. They verbalized their love for each other, and Jason drifted off. It was almost three in the morning before her parents left, and Jodie was left alone with Jason and her thoughts.

Jodie then realized that she had not notified her own lead nurse. She picked up her cell and called the cardiology unit. The night shift supervisor was very understanding and told her to take off as much time as she needed. Jodie thanked her, gave her husband a kiss, and tried to get comfortable on the couch-bed in Jason's room. She prayed again to ask her Father to give Jason and her the peace and strength to face whatever was ahead for them.

Chapter 6

Wednesday was a seemingly constant parade of staff and visitors. Dr. Hernandez and hospitalist Dr. Janice Calvert stopped by a couple of times. The neurosurgeon, Dr. Crandall Morton, reiterated what Dr. Hernandez had told them after the surgery, telling them that even though nerves had been reattached, only time would tell what the permanent damage, if any, would be. The IV medication did a good job of controlling Jason's pain.

Jason's parents, Bill and Maggie, arrived that evening. Naturally, they were concerned with their son's accident, surgery, and prognosis. Once they were assured that eventually life would be or could be near normal for Jason, they quickly reverted to their usual mode of communication, enumerating the accomplishments of Jason's older sister. Her most recent, apparently, was her being named "Realtor of the Year" for her district. Vannie had continued to grow her clientele of high-dollar sellers and buyers in the Pacific Northwest, specializing in multimillion-dollar properties. Jason's mother gave a blow-by-blow, dollar-by-dollar account of each property that Vannie had sold for or to wealthy clients during the past year. On top of that, they reported that she and her husband, Bart, had the best marriage and the most gifted, beautiful children. Jodie was glad that the drugs allowed Jason to sleep during their relating of Vannie's family vacations at Whistler, in Hawaii, and at Disneyland, and how they were planning an extended European vacation next summer. Jodie suggested that Jason's parents stay at her home while they were in town, but, of course, they wouldn't hear of it. They already had reservations at the Hilton near the airport and said they wouldn't be in the way there.

Jodie and Jason both knew, in all reality, that his parents simply preferred a place where someone was standing by to meet their every need. Both were relieved when his parents left after two hours. Jason was spent and needed to rest. Jodie also succumbed to the combined pressures of the past day and closed her eyes.

Thursday and Friday brought more of the same. There were doctor visits, nursing staff dispensing medications, checking vitals, checking input and output, lukewarm meals on a somewhat regular schedule, and housekeeping staff—emptying, wiping, cleaning, and mopping.

True to his word, Matt stopped by late Friday evening. He reported that the drive was, indeed, finished and showed Jason the pictures on his phone. The paving stones were beautifully set, exactly as Jason had designed—truly a piece of art. They had almost completed the rest of the Laurel Ridge project, with the plants and the east side retaining wall to be done by Monday evening. They should finish the last part—the mailbox area—by midday Tuesday.

On Saturday, Jason spiked a fever. Dr. Hernandez said that Jason would be staying at the hospital for at least another week and would not go home if he had a fever. He said that Jason's fever was not unusual or surprising, given the extent of his open injuries. He had started IV antibiotics while Jason was in surgery, and he now upped the dose. He discontinued his self-regulated IV narcotics in favor of oral medication; Jason was instructed to let staff know if the oral meds were not controlling his pain. He collected culture swabs from each of the incision and wound sites, and lab staff came to draw blood cultures. Jodie knew that it would be several days until those cultures were finalized.

Jodie notified her supervisor that she could probably return to work on Monday since Jason would still be there. Several of her coworkers and people from other departments came by during their breaks or lunch hours to see how Jason and she were doing. All expressed concern and offered everything from good thoughts to prayers, to mowing lawn or raking leaves, or getting anything they needed. Jodie made a quick trip home each morning to shower and promptly returned to be with Jason.

Kristen stopped by daily for a few minutes. Jodie prayed that Kristen's responses might be indicators that she was beginning to have a change of heart and that the healing of her relationship with the family might begin.

Kristen had essentially turned her back on the faith in which she was raised and had led a life of self-gratification, with little thought concerning God or her family. Her current relationship with Peter was no secret, and he was only the most recent in a string of relationships in which she had given freely of herself. Each of those relationships had lasted only a short time—the longest being no more than six months and the shortest being a few hours. Her anger toward God continued to fester. She blamed God for her failures in securing a career in New York. Upon her arrival back in Crescent Valley, Kristen had been encouraged to return to college and get a degree that could stabilize her future. Her parents, she felt, were attempting to run her life. She had let it be known that she was in charge and that no one was going to tell her what to do. At that time, she determined that she would not go to college or do anything that even slightly resembled something her parents might approve.

Kristen viewed her younger sister as her rival. Jodie was the good one—the one who went to college, the one who found the perfect husband, the one who landed a wonderful job, the one who had a house, the one who shared her parents' faith. Nothing ever went wrong for Jodie; everything always worked out for her. That rivalry resulted in Kristen keeping her distance from her sister. She had refused invitation after invitation to join Jodie in various activities, since she had returned earlier in the year.

A small part of Kristen was glad that something had finally gone wrong for Jodie. It rather shocked her that the thought had come into her head. Guilt soon overtook the thought, and she promptly justified the initial thought. Kristen had determined a long time ago that guilt was not going to be a part of her life. Yet here it was again. She had desperately tried to rid herself of that unwelcomed emotion. She had resolved that she would be strong and in control. She would help her sister for now, but she wasn't about to give up control.

Chapter 7

S leeping on the makeshift bed, the hustle and bustle of the unit, the familiar sounds of hospital caregiving, and the concern for her husband had not allowed Jodie the restorative rest she needed. She awoke Sunday morning feeling a bit nauseous. When Jason's breakfast arrived, that feeling intensified.

"You need to go get something to eat too," Jason urged his wife. "Your stomach will feel better when you get something into it."

Jodie smiled. "There you go again—playing doctor."

"And I am getting pretty good at it. I think I may be right again."

"Maybe so. I will go and see what I can find." Jodie kissed him and made her way to the cafeteria.

Nothing that she saw looked appealing to her, but she finally settled for two pieces of wheat toast and a cup of hot ginger tea. Wrapping the toast in a napkin, she hurried back to Jason's room.

Jason had finished eating his cheese omelet and bacon strips by the time Jodie pulled her chair up to the bed and ate her toast. That, along with the tea, did seem to calm her stomach.

"It is you!" A voice from the open door startled the couple.

Jodie looked up to see Selma enter the room. Jodie and Selma had come to Crescent Valley Memorial at about the same time three years ago. They both had been assigned to the swing shift on the med-surg unit. They had enjoyed working together for about six months before the hospital changed to twelve-hour shifts for most of the nursing staff. At that time, Selma went to orthopedics, while Jodie took an opening in the cardiac unit.

"It's me. Selma, this is my husband, Jason." Jodie motioned toward the bed. "Jason, this is Selma. Do you remember my talking of her when I first started here?"

"Yeah, I remember that name. I'm glad to meet you." Jason extended his hand.

Selma took it. "I glad to meet you as well, but I wish the circumstances were better. From what I learned when I came on duty this morning, you have had a pretty rough go of it."

"I've been better, for sure. It does help to have a full-time private nurse." Jason winked at Jodie.

"Well, I am working down at the other end today, but I just had to stop by. I'll check back later when I get a chance." Selma gave a little wave and went back to her work.

Sunday afternoon and evening proved to be challenging times for Jason. His parents stopped in as they had each day and stayed for an hour or so. While Jason was pleased that they had come, he was not surprised or particularly unhappy when they announced that they had a 6:00 a.m. flight Monday to return home. They didn't want to leave Skipper, their toy poodle, in the doggie resort any longer than they had to.

Typical, Jodie thought. *That dog holds a higher priority than their own son.* She, however, could detect the added stress that their presence and his mother's constant stories brought to her husband. Their leaving would surely bring a little more peace into their lives.

They said that they would be calling to keep up with Jason's progress. They kissed and hugged their son and said their goodbyes. Again, Jason took advantage of a nap after their departure.

Upon awakening, Jason appeared rather distraught. It seemed that the reality of his situation was beginning to sink in. He realized that the recovery ahead would be long and hard. He was not going to be able to go to the work sites to see the landscaping projects, let alone be able to work alongside his crew and make sure everything was done correctly.

Jodie could see the distress and concern that clouded his usually bright eyes.

"Jason, what's going on?" she asked tenderly. "I mean what's going on—beyond your physical body?"

Jason looked toward the ceiling, and for the first time since the accident, tears filled his eyes.

"What is it, sweetheart?" Jodie took his hand.

"I was just thinking of the future—our near future—like the next year. What is going to happen to the business? Is Matt going to be able to keep it going? Will the reputation of the company that I have worked so hard to build be maintained? Will we be able to get any new projects without my getting out there? Am I going to have to lay off some guys?" The concern spread over Jason's whole face as he spoke.

"Oh, Jason, you sound like a promotion for the next episode of a continued story. I know it is scary, but we will make it through." Jodie took a long, deep breath. "God will bring us through. Matt will do an excellent job. He won't let you down. I heard it in the way he talked." The words flowed from her mouth, and inwardly, she hoped they were true.

Chapter 8

Jodie woke very early Monday morning and went home to shower and dress for work. Her stomach again was a bit queasy. She chalked it up to what her body had endured, her lack of sleep, and returning to work. She grabbed a piece of buttered toast and hurried back to the hospital so she could spend a few moments with Jason before her shift began.

Jodie fell easily into her work routine, but her mind was continually with Jason. She had asked him to call and give her an update as soon as the doctor had made his rounds. She ran to his room to see him during her break. She couldn't wait for her lunchtime so she could spend more time with him.

At lunch, Jodie was pleased to learn that Pastor Ron had come that morning. Jason reported that he had told Ron of his concerns about the business. The pastor had prayed with him and assured him that he would be, in his words, "walking this journey with them." He also said he would ask others at the church to come by, as they were able, when Jodie was working. Jodie was grateful for good friends like Ron and Sylvia.

One of the wound cultures that had been collected on Saturday grew a Staphylococcus organism, the probable cause of Jason's fever. The bacteria, the lab reported, was sensitive to the antibiotic that Jason had been receiving, so it would already be working to kill off this attack in his body. Thankfully, the blood cultures were negative. Jodie knew they should soon be seeing a drop in his fever.

Even though her afternoon was quite busy, Jodie could not keep her eyes off the clock and her mind off her husband. Finally, her shift ended. Back in Jason's room, she downed a vending machine ham and cheese on wheat and a bag of Cheetos. She was glad to learn that her parents had stopped in. Her dad was going to meet with Matt tomorrow to discuss the projects that Jason had already secured, the ones waiting on bid acceptance, and leads that had not yet been assessed for bids.

Jason remarked that Matt had called to say that the Laurel Ridge project was completed. They had been able to get the mailbox area done by working a few extra hours. He had also emailed photos of the project and the check he was given. Tomorrow, the crew would be moving onto the Crescent Hollow job, the one with the backyard water feature and paver patio. In comparison to the one they had just finished, it was a smaller project, and they expected it to take only two days.

The update on the business and the news that the crew was seemingly doing well served to brighten Jason's spirits considerably. His fever, too, was almost gone, causing him to feel better physically.

Jason recounted his first physical therapy session, which brought new pains to his body. He had not realized how just a few days of not using certain muscles could make them so stiff. Nor had he realized that a petite physical therapist could push his foot into angles that could produce so much, as she had put it, "discomfort." Even though he had a certain amount of numbness in his left leg, he was amazed that it could hurt so much.

Jodie smiled. "I'll ask them to give you something before your next session that will ease that discomfort. You might need a little something extra to get you through PT for some time."

The days that followed were much the same for both Jason and Jodie. Jodie would dash home in the morning and get ready for work. Jason would endure more therapy, get to know more staff, and eat hospital food. He learned to order the food that was designed to be eaten cold, rather than being disappointed with warm food that should have been hot. On Thursday evening, Pastor Ron brought a Carnivore Crash, Jason's favorite pizza from Crescent Castle. *How did he manage to keep it hot?* Jason wondered, but he was unable to get the question out of his mouth before the first bite of pizza went in. "That"—Jason swallowed—"is the best thing I have tasted in more than a week!"

As promised, Jason's parents called to check on his progress, although it seemed they only had time to check in every other day. The conversations lasted only a few minutes since his mother did not want to hear the boring landscaping business talk or the gory details of his recovery and therapy. Beyond that, she talked of their busy social schedule.

Dr. Hernandez, on Friday, commented on how well Jason was doing and said that he thought they could begin planning to go home next Monday or Tuesday. Jason would still need to have someone with him twenty-four hours a day, and they would need to have a hospital bed on the first floor. Jodie felt a bit overwhelmed as she started making plans for Jason's homecoming. She knew she had enough paid time off to last about two more weeks and another two weeks of emergency paid leave. After that, they would be on their own.

Could they find someone to stay with Jason so she could go back to work? Would their insurance cover his in-home care? Could she trust Jason's care at home to anyone else? How would she get him to his outpatient follow-up appointments? The questions flooded Jodie's brain. How was she going to get through all of this?

"I've got to get organized!" Jodie said to Jason.

"Since when have you not been organized?" he queried.

"All of these things that I have to get settled before you come home," she replied. "I have to know what we are going to do."

"Sweetie." Jason smiled at his wife. "Listen to me. My body is really messed up right now, but my brain is not broken. Let me help with that list that I know you are about to compile. I can still use a phone."

"You're right."

"Okay, let me have it. What is first?"

The two of them worked their way through the list of things that had to be done, deciding which Jason could arrange online or by phone and which Jodie would do.

"Now," he said, grinning, "what's left?"

"The hard questions are what's left. Once you come home, I will not be able to work, and I will soon use up all my available paid time off. And Dr. Hernandez already said that there will be more surgeries in the coming year. I know your business will continue, but the crew will not be able to match the income level that you did. Oh, Jason," she said, her voice trembling, "how are we going to pay for everything?"

"Hey, hey there." Jason pulled Jodie to him. "I forgot to tell you. Our insurance agent called today. The other driver's insurance will be paying all our hospital and extended recovery expenses. They will also be paying for lost wages for me and will be paying you to provide twenty-four-hour live-in care for as long as I need it. He is going to bring over the expense forms this afternoon."

Jodie's mouth gaped open. "You're kidding!" She paused. "You're not kidding?"

"I'm not kidding. There are some limitations, but we should be okay."

"Oh, Jason!" She clasped her hand over her mouth.

"And," he continued, "his insurance will be covering replacement of the truck."

Jodie grabbed a tissue and wiped her eyes. "Really? Really, Jason?"

"Yup! Really!" He grinned at his wife. "Apparently, the driver of the SUV was caught on the red-light camera—with his cell phone at his ear. His insurance company did not balk at all to paying the expenses."

"I can scarcely believe it!" She let out a long breath. "That means that I can stay at home and take care of you."

Jodie felt weak in her knees, and she sank into the chair.

"I still am concerned for my crew though. I have enough jobs to sustain them all for another few weeks, but I need to follow up on a couple of bids I have out. Then I will need to get some new bids out there to secure some more work." Jason rubbed his hands together. "Matt is good, but besides not having the time to do it, he does not have any experience in giving bids. I am just not sure how I am going to be able to get that done."

"How much do you think I could help with that?" Jodie asked, still forming the thought in her brain.

"What?" Jason snapped his head toward his wife. "My wife, who is a nurse, will go out and bid my landscaping projects? Matt is not ready yet, but at least he knows the difference between cottage stone and concrete block. Do you how many years it took me to get my quotes right? And even now, there are times that I still mess up on a bid."

"Just hear me out, Jason," Jodie answered. "What I was thinking was that …" She briefly paused. "Perhaps I could go and see the project and take pictures and videos. We could FaceTime or Skype the project with the client, so you could ask anything that you would normally ask him or her in person."

Jason brought the thumbnail end of his fist to his mouth and thumped it thoughtfully. "You know, that might actually work. At the least, they would have a more attractive bidder."

"That would probably depend on if the client was a he or a she."

"Yeah, and you could take the tape measure so I could get any measurements that I would need," Jason responded, still pondering the details. "The wonders of modern technology—and to think this could work!"

"And you could still do your own calling to line up new projects to bid. You can just tell them that you will be sending your bright assistant out to gather the data for the bid." Jodie smiled.

"Bright indeed! You are the one who came up with this brilliant plan."

Chapter 9

J odie kept busy Saturday and Sunday, securing a hospital bed with an overhead trapeze bar, a special reclining wheelchair, and other necessities for Jason's homecoming. With help from her parents and the rental facility, they rearranged the family room to provide a first-floor bedroom for him. Satisfied that the room would meet their needs, she took time to do some grocery shopping—something she had not done for several weeks since she had been eating all her meals at Crescent Valley. She made sure that she included many of Jason's favorites, and she knew she would be serving them piping hot.

She had called her manager and arranged for medical leave for at least four weeks. Her manager reiterated that she should take all the time she needed. She had also started taking home the flowers and cards that had accumulated in Jason's room.

On Monday morning, Jason's heparin drip was discontinued, and plans were made to remove the IV port from his arm. The night before, he had been given an oral anticoagulant, which would keep his body from forming blood clots. He was told that a home physical therapist would be making regular visits. He was glad that Jodie was a nurse and could navigate through all the medical terminology and assist so much in his recovery. Dr. Hernandez stated that he was letting Jason go home earlier than most because of her being able to be there to provide care for him. If it were not for Jodie, he would have had to go to a rehab facility. It brought Jason a deep sense of confidence in this transfer home.

Jodie, on the other hand, was not so confident. Even though Jason's vital signs had been very stable, and his day-to-day care was, for the most part, routine—this was Jason. She would have total responsibility for his care, and she wouldn't have a call button to summon assistance. What if she did something wrong? As she thought of disaster possibilities, her stomach churned. She was sure that once they were home and had established a routine, her stomach problems would go away. There always seemed to be one more thing on her mind that caused her an uneasy stomach. She wondered if this was an indication that she was not trusting God as fully as she ought to be.

Dr. Calvert wrote the discharge orders on Tuesday morning, and Jason's transportation to their home was arranged. A friend had loaned Jodie his customized van for as long as she needed it; he had taken Jodie's Subaru in exchange. The staff taught Jason and Jodie how to get in and out of the reclining wheelchair. Specialized straps held the wheelchair in place in the van. Jodie's dad took the steering wheel of the van, and with Jodie riding shotgun, Jason securely strapped down in back, and Bonnie following behind, the trek home began.

When they got to their house in Crescent Mound, they were quite surprised to find Kristen waiting for them.

"Thought you might need an extra pair of hands," she said, greeting them.

Jason and Jodie were grateful for Kristen's help. Even though they were busy getting things into place, Jodie could tell that her sister was distracted and on edge. Finally, everything was set up. Jason had his laptop, phone, TV remote, a big glass of ice-cold lemonade, and his favorite tortilla chips all within reach. Those adjustable tray tables really made things easier. What more did a man need? Okay, maybe to be able to get out of bed by himself, go to the bathroom by himself, take a shower, dress, and walk— yeah, some of those things. They all knew it would still be some time before any of those would be possible.

"Are you sure you are going to be all right on your own?" Bonnie asked.

"I hope so." Jodie smiled with teeth clenched and a slight shrug of her shoulders.

"We are just a phone call away, and we can be here in minutes."

Her mother gave her a hug, as did her father.

"We'll stop by after work tomorrow, but don't hesitate to call either or both of us when you need anything during the day," Dale added.

Jodie smiled and nodded. "Thank you so much—for everything."

Her parents headed to their car, and Jodie joined her sister in the kitchen.

"Would you like a glass of lemonade, sis?" Jodie asked as she reached for two glasses from the cupboard.

"That would be nice."

Even though their relationship and conversations had been stilted and superficial for several years, Jodie couldn't help but notice that Kristen was distraught.

"Is everything okay?" Jodie probed.

"No." Kristen brought her hand to her mouth, and tears brimmed in her eyes.

Jodie pulled out a chair and sat down. Motioning to another chair, Jodie said, "Sit. Let's talk."

Kristen took a deep breath and said, "I guess there is no way to get this out except to say it. I don't want Mom and Dad to know this yet. Okay?"

"As long as my keeping quiet does not endanger your life or someone else's, I'll keep quiet." Jodie reached out her hand.

"Okay." After another deep breath and a slow exhale, Kristen began. "First of all, I'm pregnant. I didn't mean for it to happen, but it did."

Jodie squeezed her sister's hand. Even though Jodie knew that Kristen had not been celibate, hearing the news still was a shock. "Oh, Kristen— are you sure?"

Kristen nodded. "Yes, I'm sure. For a couple of weeks, I thought I might be, so I bought one of those tests yesterday. It was positive."

"We'll make it through this," Jodie assured her sister. Now it was her time to take a deep breath. "We are still family, and family is there for each other."

"I wish I could say the same for Pete." Kristen sobbed. "I told him last night, and he got mad—I mean, really mad! I've never seen him so upset."

"He probably just needs some time to get used to the idea." Jodie got up and pulled her sister close.

"No, he stormed out of the apartment, and he told me—no, yelled at me—that I knew that was never a part of the deal. I did know that. I didn't mean for it to happen. He had always said that he didn't want kids—ever!

I knew that. I was hoping that he might change his mind since now there really is a baby."

Jodie grabbed a box of tissues and set them on the table.

Kristen took a couple and blew her nose. "When Pete left, he told me to pack my stuff and be out by the end of the week. He called me irresponsible and told me to just get rid of it."

"We'll be there for you, Kristen, and for your baby." Jodie looked deeply into her sister's eyes. "We'll make it through this."

"How could I have been so wrong about Pete?" Kristen sobbed again. "He told me we were absolutely through and that I could also start looking for another job. How could he do this?"

"Do you love him?" Jodie queried.

"I don't know, but it was working. I thought we had had something that could grow into love. We were both free spirits. You know—live and let live. He said that I had betrayed his trust, and he wanted nothing more to do with me—that he never wanted to see me again after I was out."

"What do you need right now? Do you need a place to stay?"

"Yeah, I will. I guess I will also have to tell Mom and Dad." Kristen counted off the items on her fingers. "And I will need a job. And I need to move my stuff out of Pete's place. And I will need prenatal care. I don't have any insurance. How am I going to raise a baby on my own?"

"I said it before. We will get through it together."

"Thanks, sis. I certainly don't deserve this from you."

Jodie mulled over the irony of the situation. Jason and she so longed for a baby, and now Kristen had an unplanned and unwanted pregnancy. She moved into her organizational mode and grabbed a pen and paper. "Okay, let's get everything on a list. One, tell Mom and Dad. When do you want to do that?"

"I don't know."

"I think it should be soon, so we can all work together and not have to hide things."

"They are going to be so upset. They might join Pete and decide they never want to see me again. But you are right; the sooner I tell them, the sooner I will know what I am facing."

Jodie nodded sympathetically. She was not sure how her parents would react. She was sure that they had already recognized that this might be a possibility, given Kristen's chosen lifestyle. "I think they will help. Just give them the opportunity."

"Yeah, I hope you are right. I need to tell them tomorrow."

"Task one—check!" Jodie made a checkmark on the paper, and Kristen smiled.

"You and your lists!"

"Well, it works for me," Jodie responded. "Ready for number two?"

Kristen had regained her composure a little. "I guess that would be to find a place to stay—for a while anyway, and then a more permanent place."

"Two—a place to live. Since Jason is downstairs, for now, you could stay here until you find another place. Of course, I don't want you to be bringing in guys or creating any drama for us. Jason needs a calm recovery place."

"I can't believe you even said that!" Kristen blurted out.

"I don't want to upset you, but I wanted to make sure that you understood the values that we have for our home. They are not exactly the same values that you have embraced," Jodie explained.

"I know. I guess I deserved that." Her voice softened. "I shouldn't have reacted that way. I am so emotionally unstable right now. I know that you have not approved of the way I have been living. While I am with you, I promise that I will abide by your house rules."

"Check. Why don't you go get what you need from Pete's, and I'll get our guest room ready for you? I need to check in on Jason and make sure he is doing okay." Jodie stood to usher her sister to the door.

"Do you think that it will be okay with Jason—I mean, my staying here?" Kristen paused at the door.

"There is no one who takes helping others more seriously than Jason. I know that he will be okay with it."

"Thank you, little sis," said Kristen as she gave Jodie a hug. "I will be back in a couple of hours."

Chapter 10

Jodie took care of Jason's needs and explained the situation into which Kristen had gotten herself. Jason was understanding, but he was also a bit skeptical of bringing her into their home. *Rightfully so*, thought Jodie. Kristen had not proven herself to be a person who would readily change her lifestyle or who cared much about anyone besides herself. She had, however, been quite helpful since Jason's accident.

"And," Jodie added, "having her here would be good if I need to run some errands."

"Okay, we'll do it. I don't want her stay here to be prolonged. Making it a long-term solution will not really be helpful to Kristen." Jason's voice sounded firm.

Jodie nodded. "We didn't set up a tight limit yet, but she will need to have time to land a new job and find a place to live."

"Yeah, I can see that. I guess it is time that we put some feet to our faith and help someone in need. It just seems easier to help a stranger on the street or a needy child in a third world country than to extend that help to someone in the family who has been deliberately and consistently making bad decisions." He took another sip of lemonade. "When she gets back, let's sit down together and get it all out on the table."

"Well, Kristen and I will sit down. You will lie there." She grinned. "I want to think that Mom and Dad will not go haywire when Kristen tells them."

"Your parents will not be happy, for sure, but I don't think they will be any more unhappy with this news than they are already with her general choices in life. Maybe this is what it will take for Kristen to get her life turned around. I would like to think that they will help as needed."

When Kristen returned, she brought a big gray backpack and three large black trash bags full of her belongings. "I didn't have any luggage or boxes—at least these are a matched set." She pointed to the bags.

Jodie nodded. "I have the guest room ready for you upstairs. You can put your stuff in the drawers, and I put some hangers in the closet for you."

"Thanks, but I don't own many hanger-type clothes," said Kristen as she made her way up the stairs with two of the bags. In a few minutes, she was back down to retrieve the third bag and the backpack.

"I didn't bring any groceries because I didn't want Pete to accuse me of stealing his food," Kristen said as she came into the kitchen. "Smells good!"

"It is the same meal I made for Jason the day of the accident."

"Yum—that was good! By the way, thanks for that meal. Pete really liked it too."

"Oh yeah, I forgot that I had you take it. This should be better, as it won't be so dried out. This is one of Jason's favorites, and I wanted his first meal home to be one he really likes," Jodie said as she opened the oven door. "Mm—can't wait."

Kristen helped Jodie move the meal to the family room where Jason's bed had been set. Jason raved about the meal. "I think I would say this even if I had not been eating almost two weeks of mediocre hospital food, but this is one of the best you have ever done, my love!"

"Thank you, Jason." Jodie beamed as she stooped to kiss her husband.

After the meal, the three of them discussed the conditions for Kristen's stay. Because she was in no position to object, Kristen acquiesced to all the terms, including "no Pete" or any other men at the house. That, she maintained, would not be a problem as, even if she should want to talk to him—which she did not—she was quite adamant that he was absolutely finished with her.

Bonnie called to check on how things were going. Jodie didn't tell her about Kristen being there. No, that was Kristen's job. Jodie asked that her parents come by for dinner the next evening, and she would make lasagna. Bonnie said she would bring a salad and a chocolate cake. This would give Kristen one day to prepare to tell their parents—item number one on the Kristen-stabilization checklist.

Chapter 11

Kristen started her job hunt—item number three. Why hadn't she gone back to college and made herself more job ready? Why had she locked herself into the unskilled category of low-paying jobs? Why did she make so many mistakes? She continued the self-deprecating questions as she drove from one place to another—coffee shops and cafes, grocery stores and mall shops, and even the hospital. She made inquiries, filled out three applications, and was told numerous times that there were no current openings. She was told by one shop near the mall that they might have some seasonal Christmas hours beginning mid-November. The fact that tonight she would face her parents weighed heavily on her mind. She was exhausted, more mentally and emotionally than physically, when at 3:00 p.m. she made her way back to Jodie's house.

It wasn't until she arrived that she realized that she hadn't eaten anything all day.

"How'd it go?" asked Jodie as Kristen walked through the door.

"Fantastic!" Kristen looked askance at her sister. "I have an interview tomorrow for CEO of Dutch Brothers."

"I'm glad you are able to make a joke!"

"In all reality? Nothing." Kristen sighed. "I bet I stopped by ten places, and I completed some applications, but none look promising. Even if I should get one of them, they hardly pay enough for me to live, let alone provide for a baby."

"Have you given any thought to going back to school?" Jodie inquired.

"Yes, Mom—oh, I'm sorry, Jodie. I guess I am just so touchy about that area." Kristen wiped her hand across her forehead. "Do you have something that I could eat?"

"As long as you are staying here, you are welcome to eat anything we have. You don't need to ask."

"You're a good sister, Jodie—better than I deserve." Kristen opened the refrigerator and spotted some key lime yogurt. She took a bite.

"This is really good. Thanks!"

"I wasn't quite sure of the flavor when I bought it, but I think it's great too," Jodie responded.

"Actually, I have been beating myself up all day, wishing that I had made different choices in my life." Kristen sat down at the table. "I realized that I do not have any marketable skills to land a job that pays enough to support me and my baby. About school—I don't have any money for that either."

"If you had the money, what would you study?" Jodie asked.

"Do you know of any place that offers a major in barista-ing with a minor in modern art or fashion?"

"No, but I am thinking that you might do pretty well owning an artsy coffee shop. What would you think about taking courses toward a business major? They would probably offer classes in entrepreneurship that could be of help." Jodie raised her eyebrows as she questioned her sister.

"Even if I did, I don't have any way of paying for courses." Kristen looked down into her yogurt.

"There may be a way," Jodie continued. "I know of some single moms at the hospital who were able to get some tuition assistance. I don't know how they got it, but I could find out if you are truly interested."

"I would be interested—I mean, I am interested." Kristen looked up.

"Am I hearing you say that you are actually considering another stint at school?" Both giggled.

"I'll make some calls this afternoon and see what I can find out for you." Jodie laid her hand on her sister's shoulder. "Would you like to help me make the lasagna?"

"It's the least I can do; you have been such a help to me."

Jodie made her calls and found out that Kristen could make an appointment at the local community college to find out about the low-income tuition-assistance program. She told Jason about her newfound knowledge.

"Just make sure that she takes it from here, Jodie," he cautioned. "She needs to take the initiative on these things."

"I know. It's just that on this, I knew a couple of people who had gotten assistance, and I was just finding out how they went about it and where Kristen should start."

"Well, again," he reminded, "be cautious. When you start saying 'it's just' or 'I was just,' it sounds like you are trying to justify your doing the work. By the way, bright, young landscaping assistant," Jason continued, "do you think you might be up to your doing first quote trip this Friday?"

"Yeah! At least I think so. Do you have something?"

"Almost," he replied. "I've been on the phone with this guy who has a riding stable and wants to do a major project with a fountain and rock creek at the entrance. So my next step will be to send you out."

Jodie grinned broadly. "I'm your go-to person! I can't believe it, but I really am excited about doing this."

Jodie was more than a little nervous as she greeted her parents at the door. They were surprised but pleased to see Kristen. "We didn't expect to see you here tonight," her dad said as he looked at his oldest daughter.

Kristen nodded. "Yeah, I, uh, have some things to discuss, but we can wait until dinner."

Chapter 12

After the dinner was set on the table and, from his bed, Jason had said a prayer, Dale broached the subject. "Well, Kristen, what's up?"

Kristen took a long, deep breath. "Dad? Mom? This is unbelievably hard, and I'm not sure where to start."

"Usually, it is best just to start. The starting place is not so important once you get started," her dad responded, concern heavy in his voice.

"Okay. I don't want to hurt you guys because I really do love you both."

"We know you do, honey." Bonnie got up from her chair and moved toward her daughter.

After another deep breath, Kristen continued, "First of all, and the most major part, is that I am pregnant."

Bonnie put her arm around Kristen and laid her head on her daughter's head.

"Secondly, Pete tossed me out, and he doesn't want this baby or me at all. I didn't mean for this to happen, but it did."

Dale joined his wife. "Kristen, we love you, and there is nothing that could ever change that. When we take chances, sometimes things happen that we didn't plan. We can tell that this pains you tremendously, and we share in your pain."

"We will get through this, Kristen," Bonnie added. "God can always bring good out of seemingly bad situations."

Kristen dissolved into tears. Between sobs, she shared how she now had no job, no place to live, and a baby on the way. She told of her day of looking for a job and her thoughts about going back to school and eventually, perhaps, owning her own coffee place. The more she talked, the more composed she became. Her voice became stronger as she said how she would be staying with Jodie for a while.

As everyone sat back down and resumed their meal, Dale asked, "Is that going to work out for you, Jodie? Jason?" He looked from one to the other.

"Yes, Dad. Jason, Kristen, and I had a good discussion on how this is going to work. I think we have a plan in place, and we have set ground rules. In a way, it may be helpful to have someone else here—it will give me a little more peace of mind, especially at night or when I have to go out for something." Jodie smiled at her sister.

"Jodie," Kristen said, smiling back, "you make it sound like I am doing you a favor when it is so much the other way around. I can't believe you are being so kind to me after the way I have treated you the past few years."

"I've been learning a lot about grace the past few years—both in receiving it and giving it," Jodie responded.

"I want you to know, Kristen," Bonnie interjected, "that you also can have a home back with us at any time."

Kristen picked up her napkin and wiped her eyes. "I was so afraid of telling you; so afraid that you would be mad at me; so afraid that you would push me away as Pete did."

With eyes full of compassion, Dale responded, "Kristen, many of your decisions and actions over the past ten years have, indeed, caused us much pain. We have prayed and prayed that God would bring you back. But you need to know and remember this one thing: you are our daughter and always will be our daughter. Our love for you has never wavered."

Kristen got up from her chair and wrapped her arms around her father. "You don't know what that means to me. I really don't know where I am spiritually right now. I'm not at a place to embrace God, but I can also see that I have my family back in my life to give me the support that I need right now. Thanks to all of you, maybe I can begin to stop the out-of-control spinning that has been my life ever since I found out that I was pregnant."

Jason looked at his sister-in-law. "Kristen, as I said before, we are not going to push you to any decisions that you are not yet ready to make. When you are ready to turn to God, we will be ever so glad. In the meantime, we are here to help. We will encourage you in any way we can.

We are your family, and God has placed us in your life and you in ours forever."

Her eyes again brimming with fresh tears, Kristen blubbered, "You all don't know how much each of you means to me right now."

Dale picked up the lasagna and served a piece onto his plate. "I don't know about you, but I can't resist this any longer. Jodie, this looks and smells delicious!"

"It was a joint effort," Jodie responded. "Kristen helped a lot."

The rest of the meal passed in amiable conversation, at times returning to options that were ahead for Kristen and her life.

When the dishes were cleared away and the parents had left, the sisters joined Jason in the family room.

"I think that went as well as it could, don't you?" Jodie asked her sister.

"For sure!" Kristen replied. "I had no idea how they would respond."

"What Jodie said earlier about learning about grace is true." Jason's face validated the truth of his words. "It's so easy to get judgmental. We see the way that others are living or the decisions that others are making. We try to think that we would never do this or that. In some way, we think we are better than they are. But when we come to the realization that even our best efforts are so inadequate, we get a huge helping of humility served up to us.

"And in that realization," Jason continued, "we experience the grace given to us by God. Even though there is no way that we deserve it, He gives to us freely and generously."

"Well, that is certainly what I have gotten from you guys—grace." Kristen took a breath. "I didn't deserve a place to stay, your help, or your support. You have been so generous to me."

Chapter 13

J odie pulled on a pair of her better jeans and her favorite everyday boots. Today she would interactively do her part of her first ever Igland Landscaping job quote.

Jason smiled as he watched her sweep her hair up into a ponytail and slip on a brand-new Igland Landscaping cap. Her ponytail stuck out the opening in the back. "You look almost too cute to be taken seriously, but I know you can do it."

Jodie gave her husband a warm hug and pressed her lips to his.

"I like that!" Jason responded. "I could get used to this being the procedure for doing quotes."

"Okay, I'm in. Do you want me to write a standard operating procedure for this? I'm quite experienced in writing SOPs," Jodie teased. "Now, what do I need to take with me and where do I find it?"

"You will need to take what I call my quote bag. It's the big tan canvas bag. In it are several tape measures, a notebook, a bunch of pencils, and a clipboard with sheets of the questions that need to be asked. I have already asked most of them over the phone. The bag is in my truck," Jason replied.

Jodie raised her eyebrows. "Did you forget, Jason, that the truck is no more?"

"Oh yeah." Jason slapped his forehead. "Ouch, I shouldn't have done that. My forehead is still a bit tender. The bag should be in the garage. Matt cleaned out the truck and was to have left everything there."

"I'll find it."

Jodie found the bag hanging on a hook in the garage and reviewed its contents with Jason. Jason went over the question sheet with her, emphasizing the remaining information that he needed to have to give a quote. The uneasiness in her stomach reminded her that she was so out of her comfort zone with this new role. Give her a heart valve replacement or a quadruple bypass patient any day, and she was confident of her abilities, but getting all the information for Jason to give a landscaping bid? She so needed to do a good job—no, she needed to do an excellent job for her husband. She was grateful that Jason would be on the phone with her.

"Oh, and, Jodie, why don't you go grab a couple of those magnetic Igland Landscaping signs and put them on the van doors? And while you are doing that, I will program the address into your phone." Jason took the phone Jodie held out to him.

"This one is not too far from the one we were doing at the time of the accident, and it is a similar request—except this one is much larger. The property is ten acres instead of two. The paver driveway will be longer, and the water feature larger. There will be more plants and more stonework." He handed the phone back to his wife. "It's 17114 Canyon Drive in Crescent Heights."

Jodie looked at the address and the map on her phone. "Okay, I think I have it."

"Sweetheart?" Jason looked into his wife's eyes as she lifted her gaze to him. "Watch out for the other drivers up there. Not all of them stop at stop signs."

"I will, my love!" Jodie leaned over to kiss Jason once more. "I will be sure to add this kiss to the new standard operating procedure."

Chapter 14

J odie was always amazed at the size of the homes in the Crescent Heights area. Each sat on at least two acres, and it seemed that new homes were constantly being built there. She pondered the idea that there was that much disposable wealth available in the greater Crescent Valley. She was thankful that Jason had begun to establish a reputation as an excellent landscaper in this affluent subdivision. The roads were purposely set out in winding patterns to discourage speeding through the neighborhoods. Signs reminded drivers to watch for children at play and to share the road with bicyclists. Following the directions from her phone, she turned onto Canyon Drive. She smiled as she wondered where the words "Canyon" and "Heights" had come from, as neither really existed here. The most that could be said was that there were low, rolling hills. Some developer must have come from Colorado or Wyoming and was trying to bring some of that imagery into this community.

"Here's 17114 Canyon Drive," she said to herself as she turned into the asphalt driveway. Like the road, the drive was winding, and she soon passed the stable. An expanse of white-fenced pastures flanked the property on the right. As she made another turn, she could see the house that loomed large at the end of the drive. The four-car garage gave a hint of the relative affluence of the owner. She took in the scene before her and smiled as she saw the plainness of the drive and lawn. *They really need Jason's magical touch*, she thought. Even she could begin to picture some of what Jason might be about to do with this blank slate.

She gathered the quote bag and flung it over her shoulder. "Let's do this!" she whispered to herself as she started for the front door of the house.

The door was answered by a surprisingly young man, maybe thirty-five years old at the most.

"Good morning. Mr. Tackner?"

"Please call me Craig," the man replied.

"Craig, I'm Jodie Igland." She smiled as she extended her hand. "I believe you have been speaking to my husband about a quote for your drive and some other landscaping."

"Yes, Jason and I have been talking on the phone. I am so sorry about his accident. I am pleased to be his first quote using his, as he said, bright, young assistant. So are you ready to have a go at this?" He swept his arm toward the driveway and front lawn.

"I'll just get Jason here with us on FaceTime, and we'll get started." Jodie pulled out her phone and clicked on Jason's picture. "Jason," she began, trying to use her most professional voice, "I'm here with Craig, and I am putting you on speaker phone so we can both hear you. Where would you like us to begin?"

Jason's voice came through loud and strong as he communicated from his bed. "Jodie, I need to have you get out the questions sheet and start at the top so we can review the answers that Craig has already given and get answers to the others."

Jodie got the sheet and a pencil. "Okay, Craig, let's review what you said you would like to have done here on your property. Jason has that you want the asphalt driveway replaced with pavers and focal point water features, one out near the road and another up by the stable. Both are to have fountains, and the roadside one will involve making a small pond. And you want some other interesting landscaping to bring character and interest to the grassy canvas that is now the front yard and up by your house. You said you wanted some unique plantings along the drive to the stable and some sort of horse sculpture."

Craig nodded throughout Jodie's summary of the task. He said he was counting on Jason to bring his creativity to design a showplace for them. He wanted their place to be truly one of a kind. Jason asked Craig about colors, types of plants and flowers, trees, some seating possibilities, and a host of other details. Craig said that he didn't want to give too many specifics, because he wanted Jason to use his own judgment.

As Jason and Craig went through the rest of the questions on the sheet, Jodie took careful notes. She had a good notion that Jason was also jotting down notes on his end. She was glad to find out that Craig genuinely wanted Jason's creativity. Some homeowners, she knew, had such predetermined plans that it was difficult to get them to make any changes, even when it was obvious that the existing plan would not work. This type of project, she knew, was his favorite; Craig was giving him full creative freedom.

"Okay," Jason told them, "I think I have a good idea of what you are looking for, and I have some great ideas for your property. Now I need to get down to measurements and layout. We, I mean Jodie, will be taking lots of pictures. Craig, I think I have asked everything that I need to know for now, so you can go, or you can watch Jodie take pictures and measurements. We really do appreciate your letting us get you this quote."

"I do have some things to do inside, so I think I will leave Jodie to do her thing," Craig responded. "I am glad we were able to make this work. Like I said before, my wife and I were extremely impressed with the transformation of that yard over on Spyglass Circle."

Jodie and Jason worked together to get all the measurements. Because of the property size and the length of the driveway, it took longer than she had expected. She thought about how terribly expensive it would be to do pavers on the entire drive, but she knew it would be Jason's place to present that to the client. She was, after all, just the bright, young assistant. When finished with the pictures and measurements, she rang the doorbell, confirmed Craig's email address, and told him that Jason would have the quote and the projected timeline to him within a week. Craig thanked her again.

Smiling, both inwardly and outwardly, Jodie hopped into the van and headed home. "Mission accomplished!" she said.

Chapter 15

Jason was energized by the design work he was doing for the Tackner stable project. This was the largest project he had ever done, and he knew that his success on this could lead to more work. As he sketched and revised his drawings, he could see the total picture coming together.

Jodie took the completed drawings and a contract back to the Tackners' estate. This time, Craig's wife, Rachel, joined them. Again, with FaceTime, Jason outlined all the details to the couple. Rachel, while mildly interested, did not really enter the conversation. About all she had to say was, "Just make it wonderful!" Jodie couldn't help but wonder how a couple as young as the Tackners could afford such an expensive project. When all was said and done, Craig and Rachel signed the contract. Knowing that the winter season would soon be upon them, the start and end dates were left somewhat ambiguous, with only an anticipated completion date set for the end of June. Jason's crew would be working, as weather permitted, beginning after the holidays.

Driving back down the winding Canyon Drive, Jodie again felt a wave of nausea. She pulled over to the side of the road and stepped out. Leaving her breakfast in the grassy ditch, she climbed back into the van and laid her head against the back of the seat. *That does it*, she thought. *I need to find out what is going on.*

As she neared home, she caught her breath. What if—what if she was pregnant? That made sense. It could be. That would explain both her nausea and tiredness. She couldn't believe that she hadn't thought of that possibility before. And here she was, a nurse after all. Well, it wasn't like she had had nothing else to occupy her mind for the past month. She couldn't wait to get home and share her hope with Jason. This could be one of the best days of their life. Jason had just landed his biggest contract ever—and maybe, just maybe, they were going to have a baby.

Jodie stepped on the brake as she realized that she was exceeding the speed limit as she approached their street. Apparently, more than her mind had been racing since she had left the Tackner house.

"Jason!" she shouted as she entered the house. "Guess what! I threw up on my way home from the Tackners'!"

"Well, good for you, I guess," Jason answered. "Are you okay? That is not something that a person usually gets all that excited about."

"Yes! I'm okay. I think I may be more than okay. I've been nauseous quite a bit lately, and I just figured it out. I think it's morning sickness. I think I might be pregnant." Jodie grabbed her husband's shoulders and leaned in to kiss him.

"You really think so?" Jason looked at her hopefully. "Let's find out for sure. Can you get one of those kits?"

"Yes! Let's!"

Jodie grabbed her purse and keys and drove to the nearest store to buy a pregnancy test. When she returned, she told Jason that they would look at the result together.

"Okay, here we go. Are you ready?" Jodie held the test stick in her hand.

She extended it to Jason. "Here, you hold it and turn it over on the count of three."

He took the stick, and they counted together, "One, two, three!"

As Jason turned it over, they both gasped. "Pregnant!" they shouted together as they hugged.

"I can't believe it! We're pregnant! We're going to have a baby!" Jodie's eyes brimmed with happy tears.

"Not just *a* baby—we are going to have *our* baby!" Jason pulled her down again and kissed her lips. "Let's thank God. What a day we've had!"

Together, the couple thanked God for the baby He had already given to them and for the huge landscaping job He had provided.

"When are we going to tell the family?" Jason asked.

"I think we should find out the due date first, and then we will tell them. I will call and make an appointment with an OB today." Jodie did a little dance around the bed. "We won't even tell Kristen yet. We will just have to make believe that all our joy is because of the landscaping project."

"Sounds good to me, little mama," Jason replied, with a smile that nearly took over his entire face.

Meanwhile, Kristen had accepted a seasonal job at Meyers. She had started on November 5 and had been working the night shift, stocking and cleaning. Two weeks before Black Friday, she would be moved to days and would be trained in the electronics department, where she would be employed for the remainder of the Christmas season. While she was working there, she continued her pursuit of regular employment and investigated the courses available at the community college. She enrolled in a program designed for low-income people who wanted to enter or reenter the workforce. She found out that she qualified for reduced tuition and, should she need it, childcare at "a very reasonable rate." She also discovered that she would be able to take advantage of other social services available to pregnant women and their infants. She never thought that she would be in a place of having to rely on social services, and she determined that she was going to work hard to make it on her own.

Kristen hadn't heard a word from Pete since she moved out. She did not try to contact him or tell him where she was living. *Just as well*, she thought. *I don't want him around since he made it abundantly clear that he does not want me or the baby.*

At her first appointment at the free clinic, she was given prenatal vitamins and enrolled in the WIC program that provided food during her pregnancy and after the birth of her baby.

At Jason's request, Matt joined them that evening for dinner. After devouring Jodie's honey-glazed chicken breasts and mashed potatoes, Jason went over the plans for the Tackner stable project. Matt shared Jason's enthusiasm for the project and was amazed at the creativity his boss had shown in the details. His drawings and specifications were magnificent.

"This is huge!" Matt whistled. "Wow! I can't believe the size of this!"

"I know. It's the biggest we have ever done!" Jason grinned.

Matt continued to study the plans. "When do we start?"

"Well, you should be just about finished with everything else by Christmas, right?"

"Yeah, or just a little after, but definitely by the end of December, assuming that the weather cooperates," Matt said. "I can't wait to get started on this one!"

"I told the Tackners that we would start after the first of the year, so that should work out perfectly. We will be working around the weather."

"And we could possibly have several snow removal projects dropped into the schedule any time between now and then," Matt said. "I assume we have the same contracts as last year?"

"The same, plus two more," Jason replied. "We picked up the new Crescent Lake shopping center and the retirement community off Fortieth."

"It means that we all will need to stay on top of the weather forecast. Will you be doing that, or do you want me to do it?" Matt asked.

"For right now, I will do it. God knows I need stuff to keep me busy while I am lying around," Jason answered. "How is the crew doing?"

"Pretty well. Most of them have really stepped up to the challenge of not having you there. I think they all have assumed a little more personal responsibility for making the company thrive. They want to make you proud."

"I am proud of them. They have been doing a great job." Jason rubbed his chin thoughtfully. "You said most. Is someone having a problem?"

"Sort of. It's Phil," Matt responded. "He has been late several times and seems to be making excuses for his work. He doesn't get along very well with Dave either. Dave is proving to be a good worker, and that seems to be grating on Phil. I must admit, I will usually ask Dave to do something because I know it will get done and be done right. With Phil, well, I am just not so sure."

"Let's keep an eye on Phil. Maybe I should have him stop by so we can talk things out." Jason thought out loud. "I hate to let a guy go, but I also need to make sure the crew is working well together. I'm going to call him and ask him to stop by tomorrow after work."

"Thanks, Jason." Matt nodded. "I just didn't know how to handle it myself."

Chapter 16

Reluctantly, Phil accepted Jason's invitation to come to his house the next day. He was almost sure that he was going to be fired. Sure, he had been late a few times, and his attitude had not been the best, but he was still basically a good worker. He didn't particularly care for Dave and the way he had moved ahead of him in the company. Phil's life had not been an easy one. His dad had left his mother and him shortly after Phil's fifth birthday. His mom had worked hard to provide for him, but she was seldom around. His high school years had been difficult, as he became a part of a group that had little respect for any authority. While technically not a gang, the group had a reputation of getting into trouble with the law and was prone to violent encounters. How he had escaped jail was still a mystery to Phil. The years, however, had left a mark, and he carried a large chip on his shoulder. The world, as he knew it, was not his friend, and he wasn't about to let the world win.

He had been glad to get the job with Igland Landscaping a year ago. For the first time in his life, things were going right. He worked with a good group of men. He respected Jason—one of the only people he had ever respected—and the pay was good. Even though he was usually tired after a day's work, it was a good tired. Then Dave showed up, and things began to turn south. He had to admit that Dave was good—too good. His work made Phil's work look not so good. Dave was better. Dave was faster. Dave did more. Phil felt like he couldn't compete.

Why should I? he wondered. *Why should I let the new guy get under my skin?*

The thoughts whirled in his brain as he drove to Jason's house. Should he beg for his job? He really needed it. Should he just tell Jason off and walk out? What would he do then? He couldn't afford his apartment without a job. Should he tell Jason that Matt wasn't being fair? No, if he were Matt, he would probably favor Dave as well. He knew he shouldn't have been getting to work late. He needed a plan. He had to know what he was going to do before he went in. He couldn't go in without a plan.

"Come on, man," Phil said. "Think! What are you going to do?"

He was still uncertain when he turned into Jason's drive. He rang the doorbell and was greeted by a beautiful young lady.

"Hi! You must be Phil. Jason told me you were coming," Jodie welcomed Phil. "I'm Jodie, Jason's wife. Please come in!"

"I always knew Jason was lucky in business," Phil said as he stepped inside. "It looks like he lucked out in the marriage department as well."

Jodie blushed, and Phil immediately apologized. "I'm sorry. I shouldn't have said that. It wasn't an appropriate thing to say to the wife of my boss."

"Oh, no worry," Jodie stammered as she showed Phil to Jason's temporary office.

"Phil, come on in and have a seat." Jason motioned to the chair against the wall.

Phil sat down and asked, "How are you doing?"

"I've been better, and I will be better again. Right now, I am doing okay; I'm about where they think I should be. I still have a long way to go before I can walk again, but we are hopeful that I will get there."

"I hope so too," Phil said with true concern in his eyes.

Jason cleared his throat. "Phil, I wanted you to stop by so we could talk some things out. I want you to know, right off the top, that I want you to continue as a part of our crew."

"I am really glad to hear that." Phil breathed a sigh of relief. "I was afraid you were going to let me go."

"Oh, not at all! I just landed the biggest contract to date, and I need all the experienced workers I can get," Jason continued. "But there are a few wrinkles we need to iron out."

"Okay." Phil looked at his boss.

"Matt tells me there has been some tension within the crew, and it seems to be centered around you."

"That's a fair statement," Phil agreed. "I have been letting some things get to me lately. On the way here, I did a lot of thinking and realized that I should have been handling things differently."

"Good!" Jason shifted in his bed. "Here's the way I see it. You are having a problem with Dave, and that is affecting the rest of your work. Can you tell me what is going on there?"

Phil shook his head. "I really let things get to me. Dave is a good worker, and it bugged me. He works faster and better than I do. He is just plain good. I guess I got jealous when I saw Matt recognizing that Dave was doing the better job."

"I've been in this business for quite a few years now, Phil, and I have had a fair number of men work for me. None of them have been exactly the same. They all have their strengths, and all have their weaknesses, but together, we make a crew. Jealousy has no place in our crew. We all need to respect one another and value each one's contribution." Jason looked intently at Phil. "What is it that you contribute to the crew, Phil?"

"I've never thought about that," Phil responded. "But I guess, maybe, that I contribute an eye for detail—like seeing the mistake that was made in the brick design for that pool surround. And I usually have a willingness to work late."

"I agree. Those are definitely two of your strengths!" Jason nodded.

"And I guess my weakness would be the jealousy thing and using that for an excuse for being late or not working as hard as I should." Phil tipped his head back and stared at the ceiling.

"That is an honest response, Phil," Jason replied. "I appreciate that and respect you for recognizing those weaknesses. Your admission is a good step toward improvement. None of us is perfect. We will all make mistakes, but we also need to own up to those mistakes and work not to repeat them."

"I can do that, boss." Phil smiled at Jason. "I will work hard. I will not be late. I will not let jealousy ruin the best job I have ever had."

"Glad to hear it. You are a good worker and a great member of our crew. We need you, and you need us." Jason extended his hand to Phil.

Phil stood and took Jason's hand. "I feel like I just got hired all over again."

"You did!" Jason smiled.

Grinning, Phil walked to his car. His thoughts were completely different from those he had when he came. What had just happened? He had been given a second chance. He determined that he would not let Jason down.

Chapter 17

T he next week, Jodie had her appointment and found out that their baby was due in mid-May. Everything concerning her pregnancy seemed to be fine.

It was time for Jason and Jodie to invite her parents over for another meal. They made plans to call Jason's parents during the meal; he just hoped they would answer the phone. Bill and Maggie were notorious for letting the calls from their son and daughter-in-law go to voice mail. The young couple discussed the pros and cons of telling both sets of parents at the same time. They knew right off the bat that Jodie's parents would be much more excited. Jason's parents would most likely be pleased with the news but would not be overly demonstrative. They finally decided that Jason would call his parents early and set up a time for a FaceTime call, so they could tell both sets of parents at the same time.

Jason's call to his parents went about as well as he expected. They were planning to go to the country club for dinner, but they could make time for the call if it was early enough. Since there was a two-hour time difference, Jason suggested a 5:00 p.m. Pacific time for the call. That meant Jodie and he could plan dinner for 6:00 p.m. central time.

Jodie called her parents and asked them to dinner. They had said they would be glad to come, and her mom asked what she could bring.

"How about a green salad, Mom? I have plenty of dressings, but if you have time to make your homemade vinaigrette, that would be great!"

The salad with her mom's special dressing would be paired perfectly with the Swedish meatballs and noodles that she had planned. Jason suggested that Jodie also get a decorated cake that said, "We love you already, Baby Igland!"

"I like it!" Jodie grinned as she picked up the phone to call the local supermarket bakery. "I'll be back in about an hour. Anything you need before I leave?"

"I'm fine," Jason responded.

"Okay, Daddy!" Jodie kissed her husband and hurried out the door.

The air had a crisp autumn feel. *No*, Jodie thought. *More than an autumn feel—this feels like winter. It looks like it could snow.*

Kristen got up and showered. The night shift job had taken a toll on her sleep. She just couldn't seem to get enough rest. Her pregnancy, no doubt, contributed to her tiredness. She was glad she had only one more week of graveyard and then would get to sleep normal hours. Upon entering the kitchen, she saw her sister busily making her famous meatballs.

Kristen surveyed the counter. "Wow! That's a lot of meatballs! Are you expecting company?"

Jodie smiled and thought, *If you only knew that I am expecting company. In fact, he or she is already here.* But aloud, she said, "Yes, we are. I got hungry for Swedish meatballs, so I invited the folks over for dinner."

After his first taste, Dale remarked, "Wow, Jodie! I had forgotten how great your Swedish meatballs are. They certainly outrank Ikea's."

"These taste like they came straight from the old country!" Bonnie chimed.

"Well, they are basically Mormor Lindstrom's recipe," Jodie conceded. "It's my special way of remembering her."

"I miss the St. Lucia breakfast that she always did. I loved the lingonberries that she had sent directly from Sweden," Kristen added.

"She and Farfar sure had a lot of friends. Their house would be filled to the doors," Jodie smiled as she reminisced.

"I can almost taste the Swedish pancakes and the *lussebullar*," Kristen added.

"What is lussebullar?" Jason queried.

"They are delicious Swedish buns. They have saffron in them, and my mother made them only for our St. Lucia celebration," Bonnie answered.

"I remember the first time I wore the St. Lucia crown. I was so scared that my hair would catch on fire." Jodie laughed.

"Me too!" Kristen added. "I felt honored to get my chance to be St. Lucia, but I was secretly relieved when it was one of the cousin's turns. I preferred carrying the candle in my hand and following in the procession."

Jodie laughed. "Yeah, that was exactly the way I felt."

"Why don't we have a St. Lucia celebration this year?" Dale asked. "There's no reason we can't restart the Lindstrom family tradition. We could do it in memory of your parents and their lives."

"I don't think we have time to get the lingonberries from Sweden, but I bet I could get some shipped from Amazon," Jason suggested. "Let me do what I can from here so I can be a part of the preparation."

"Okay!" Bonnie clapped her hands and then grasped them in front of her. "I am so excited. Thank you, sweetheart, for the suggestion."

"And it can be my first nonmedical outing!" Jason smiled. "I will be having some changes made to my hardware, and my therapist said that I should be able to ride in a regular car and sit in a wheelchair in another few weeks."

"Jason, you didn't tell me!" Jodie hugged her husband.

"I wanted to save it for a surprise, but since we were making plans, I thought I should go ahead and let the cat out of the bag."

The family finished their meatballs and noodles. The girls cleared the dishes, and Jodie asked her sister to serve coffee to everyone. Jodie carried dessert plates and forks to the table.

Jason picked up his phone and called his parents on FaceTime. After Kristen refreshed everyone's cup, Jodie appeared with the cake, which had one burning birthday candle. Jason turned the phone so his parents could see Jodie holding the cake, and he turned on the speaker.

"A birthday?" asked Bonnie.

Kristen, Dale, and she all wore puzzled expressions.

With that, Jason and Jodie began to sing, "Happy birthday to you, happy birthday to you ..."

As they sang, "Happy birthday, Baby Igland," Jodie lowered the cake to the table, and Jason turned the phone so his parents could see the writing on the cake.

"Oh!" Bonnie squealed. "A baby!" She jumped up to hug her daughter.

Kristen sat, stunned. Again, her mind raced with questions. *What does this mean now? Are they happier about Jason and Jodie's baby than they are about mine? Will I still be welcome here?* Answers came flooding in as well. *Of course they are happier about Jodie's baby. She's married; everything is always perfect for Jodie. Jodie won't toss me out, but I do need to get my own place as soon as possible.*

Dale also stood to hug Jodie and Jason. "Congratulations, both of you! I can't believe we are going to be grandparents twice."

Kristen was relieved to hear her dad refer to her pregnancy. She snapped out of her self-talk and got up to hug her sister. "I am so glad for you. You have been wanting this for a long time."

Jason's parents added their congratulations, with his mother saying, "I'm not sure we're quite ready to be grandparents again, but I suppose we will get used to the idea."

Jason thanked his parents for their veiled congratulations.

Jodie continued with their announcement. "Our baby is due mid-May."

"You're kidding! That's the same time mine is due! The doctor at the clinic said my due date is May 10." Kristen looked around the family group while she pondered whether it would be a good or a bad thing to have both babies due at the same time.

"Our due date is the sixteenth, but, you know, babies seldom arrive on their due dates," Jodie said. "The little cousins will be very close to the same age."

"What?" Jason's mom interjected. "Kristen, you and what's his name are also expecting? I didn't know you had gotten married."

"Mom, Kristen and Pete are not married," Jason explained to his mother. "In fact, Pete and she broke up, and Kristen is living with us for right now."

"Oh," Maggie responded. "How convenient for her. Well, we have dinner plans, so we must scurry. Congratulations, Jason and Jodie. Ta-ta!"

Happy chatter continued around the table. Kristen, however, continued to mull over the implications of the two babies and their arrival dates. She knew everyone's reaction to Jodie's pregnancy was much different from the reaction to her own announcement. It seemed like this competition would never end. In fact, it would now be extended to the next generation. She determined that she would truly try to share in Jason's and Jodie's joy.

Chapter 18

Stars twinkled, and the moon was still high in the sky as the family began to awaken at 4:00 a.m. The first to rise was Bonnie, and she quickly showered prior to wakening the others. She stole a peek out the window. A dusting of snow lay on the ground, and the day promised to be clear—perfect for their celebration. It seemed good to have their girls and Jason sleeping under their roof. It almost seemed to be how she had always pictured their life to be after the girls were grown, other than Kristen not having a husband. By 4:30, she had roused the others and reminded them to make sure their bedrooms were fit to be seen.

The kids had made the trip the evening before. It was the first time that Jason had sat upright in the van since the accident. Jodie was grateful for Kristen's help in loading the wheelchair and packing the van. They had discussed returning the van to its rightful owner and getting Jodie's Subaru back. The Petersons had happily relinquished their master bedroom to Jason and Jodie, and Dale had outfitted the toilet in the ensuite with the portable height extender that the couple had brought.

Everyone was dressed by 6:00 a.m. and ready to begin the final push for the anticipated arrival of the first guests at 8:00. Everyone was grateful that the yellow lussekatter rolls, backward S-shaped lussebullar, had been made the day before. They were equally delighted that all the specially ordered items had arrived on time. The air was filled with excitement and camaraderie that the family had not experienced since before Kristen had left for New York City.

Bonnie had the coffee brewed and filled mugs for each as they arrived in the kitchen. They all knew that a good Swedish celebration had to begin with a little coffee jolt.

After Dale set up the tables and chairs, the girls spread the crisp white tablecloths, readying the tables for the holiday dishes. Seating was available for thirty people at a time. They were expecting upward of one hundred people to come through their door between eight and noon. This, Bonnie hoped, would be the beginning of a renewed family tradition to signal the start of their Christmas celebration. Mixed emotions were evident as she remembered the St. Lucia celebrations of her past, beginning with the ones she remembered that were hosted by her own grandparents, and later, by her parents. She wondered why she and Dale had not continued the tradition when her mother passed away six years ago. Maybe, at first, it was just too painful—too soon—since her mother had died three months before the first missed Swedish holiday celebration.

In the guest room, the sisters carefully arranged the nine white candles on the crown of whortleberry greens and twigs. A few weeks ago, they had found the candle frame, along with the red sash and white gowns, in a box in their parents' attic. They were delighted to see their grandmother's writing on the box, "St. Lucia gowns & crown." They had carefully washed and pressed the six gowns and hung them in the spare room, arranging the red sash on the gown to be worn by their guest of honor. Bonnie had invited thirteen-year-old Janaya Johnson, the daughter of friends from their church, to be their St. Lucia for the celebration. She would wear the white gown with the red sash and the candle wreath crown. Other invited young girls would complete the procession, each wearing a gown and carrying a white candle. The Petersons had planned that the St. Lucia procession would occur each hour. In between the procession times, everyone except St. Lucia would remove her gown and join her family for breakfast. As families came and went, the procession would include new arrivals, giving each girl an opportunity to take part. Up to five girls who were at least seven years old would be invited to be a part of each procession.

"You know, in another eight years, our own little girls could be a part of this procession," Jodie remarked as she surveyed the gowns.

Kristen chuckled. "We could both have boys."

After setting out the hand-held candles and a lighter, the two joined their mother in the kitchen.

Jason, doing his part to prepare for the guests, had already put the lingonberries into bowls and set them on the tables. Jodie watched as he moved deftly from room to room and around the tables in his wheelchair, delivering flatware to each place setting.

Jodie smiled contently as she saw her husband enjoying his ability to contribute to the festivities. "Jason, you are amazing!"

Jason grinned back. "You don't how good it feels to be up and about."

"Just don't overdo, sweetheart," Jodie continued. "I have seen way too many patients relapse due to trying to do too much too soon. And I know my husband loves to be active and involved."

"You are right. I will finish up the tables and then take a break."

"I like that idea. I think you should rest until people start to arrive."

The flurry of activity continued in the kitchen as Bonnie directed her small crew. By seven thirty, everything was ready except for the Swedish pancakes, which would be made fresh as guests were seated. The plan was that Kristen and Jodie would be the servers and table clearers, while Bonnie and Dale took turns making the pancakes. Jason would help by greeting the guests and keeping an eye on what needed to be replenished on the tables.

Right on time, Janaya, their St. Lucia, arrived. Kristen ushered her into the guest room and assisted her in changing into the gown. She carefully placed the wreath crown on the young girl's head, smoothing her blonde hair. She took Janaya to the kitchen and handed her the basket of rolls, showing her where and how to refill her basket. After she was certain that the crown and candles were secure, she lit the candles.

"How do you feel?" Kristen asked.

"A little nervous," Janaya replied.

"About the candles or about the procession and giving out the rolls?"

"Both, I think. But more nervous about the candles."

"I know exactly how you feel. I felt the same way my first time. I was only ten." Kristen patted the back of her charge. "Don't worry! In all the years that my grandparents did the celebration, they used this same wreath frame, and no one ever caught on fire—not even close." Kristen extinguished the candles.

"What happens when the candles burn down?" Janaya asked, still unconvinced.

"The candles burn quite slowly, and we will replace them before each procession. Trust me—it will be okay. We make sure that they are good and secure."

The two returned to the guest room just before people started arriving and four younger girls, directed by Jason, came into the room. Kristen slipped gowns on the girls and gave them each a candle. After giving instructions, Kristen lit the candles on the crown and in each of the girls' hands. She stuck her head out of the door to signal to her father that the group was ready. She heard her father announce, "Welcome to our home and to our St. Lucia breakfast. Please welcome St. Lucia!" That was her cue, and she motioned for the procession to begin. With her basket of lussekatter rolls, St. Lucia, followed by her candle-carrying entourage, made her way to the living room.

The "oohs" and "aahs" filled the space as Lucia appeared with her flaming headpiece. She greeted each guest with a smile and, "Gud Jul!" Janaya quickly fell into her role. Her parents raved about her performance, and each gave her a hug, being careful to avoid the flames. "We are so proud of you," her mother whispered. Janaya responded with a wide grin. Following the procession through the dining room and the family room, the girls in the procession walked back to the guest room. Assisted by Kristen, the girls removed their gowns and carefully rehung them on the hangers. Kristen and Jodie had agreed to take turns assisting with the procession. The procession girls joined their parents, where they were served a roll, followed by Swedish pancakes.

The day went smoothly, with each procession beginning on the hour. Matt and others from the landscaping crew arrived at about ten thirty. As she poured the coffee and served them their pancakes, Kristen couldn't help but notice Matt's rugged good looks. She was also captivated by his quiet, polite demeanor. At one point, she found herself staring at him from the kitchen door. Those eyes, as blue as the cloudless sky outside, glanced her way, and she quickly turned to grab a carafe of coffee. She purposely started her service with the table in the family room, the farthest from where Matt was seated in the living room. No, she was not interested in him. She was not interested in any man—not after the way Pete had treated her and her baby. As she expected, there had not been any attempt at communication from Pete, and Kristen was not eager to resume that relationship in any way, shape, or form. What a difference between the boisterous, self-consumed Pete and the mild-mannered Matt.

By the end of her morning, Janaya was reasonably exhausted. One never would have noticed though, as she continued to be a most enchanting St. Lucia. Shortly after noon, Jodie helped her from her gown and removed the crown. "Well? What did you think?"

"I loved it!" she responded. "It was the most fun I have ever had."

"The most fun?" Jodie raised her eyebrows at the young lady.

"Well, it hit the top ten anyway. I felt so grown-up, and I loved playing the part. I would love to do it again next year."

"Maybe, but our family tradition is that the role of St. Lucia gets passed around. You never know, though, because she is usually at least ten to twelve years old and has had a few years' experience in the procession," Jodie explained. "As you discovered, having the candles on your head is a bit unnerving, and greeting people for hours is tiring."

"I understand, but if you need an experienced St. Lucia next year, please give me a call," Janaya said as she hurried to eat a roll and some Swedish pancakes of her own.

After all the guests had left, the family collapsed on the couches in the family room.

"That was fun!" Bonnie exclaimed. "And lots of work!"

"I agree it was a lot of work, and I am really tired, but it was every bit worth it," Dale chimed.

"Can I get you a coffee and some rolls?" Kristen asked everyone in general.

They all agreed that both sounded good, and Jodie offered to help.

"Oh, no. You just stay seated. Allow me to serve you," her sister insisted.

As she put five cups of coffee on the tray and gathered the roll basket, she wondered to herself about her unusually good mood. Was it merely because she had been a part of the reinstitution of a family tradition? Was it family itself? Was it Matt? Was it that she was beginning to change? Was God at work? Whatever it was, she knew she was happier than she had been for a long time.

Chapter 19

The next week flew by. With Jason's newfound mobility and with Jodie as his chauffeur and assistant, he was able to visit the worksite and reconnect with his crew. Being back on site invigorated him, and he drew in a deep breath of the crisp December air. Even though the weather was very unpredictable, the crew was able to complete their last project of the year. The men looked forward to the next three months of somewhat lighter work, consisting of snow removal for the Igland WinterCare clients. While the work was irregular, it provided the men with time to rest up, time to spend with family, and time to pursue their other interests. Jason always used these months to line up work for the upcoming season. In the past years since they had been married, he and Jodie had looked forward to a vacation to a warmer clime during the chilly winter. This year, they had planned a February Hawaii trip, but those plans had to be deferred due to the accident. There was next year, but next year they would have a baby with them. That would certainly change a Hawaiian vacation.

Jason mulled over the options for a trip this winter. Maybe they could go somewhere a bit closer and not so long. He knew he had further surgery planned in just four to five weeks, and there would be recovery time. And there would be more physical therapy—always more physical therapy. No, it didn't look like there would be much of a vacation this season. They would just have to make the best of it.

Jason picked up his laptop and went online to do his Christmas shopping for Jodie. Shopping was never a real pleasure for Jason, but when it came to shopping for something special for his wife, it always seemed fun. He thought back over the months since the accident and all that Jodie had done for him, both as his nurse and as his wife, not to mention her work as his bright, young assistant. What a kind heart and willing spirit she had. Her main Christmas gift had to be extraordinary, but he really didn't have a clue as to what he would get. Why had he waited so long? Oh, yeah, he was a guy, and guys always waited until the last minute to buy gifts. And then there was the accident—that had certainly slowed him down a bit.

Jason perused his options. "Jewelry? All ladies like jewelry, right?" But Jodie didn't wear much jewelry. She couldn't wear it at work—other than her rings, watch, and earrings, and she seldom wore anything more than that the rest of the time. She was more of a blue jeans gal. No, jewelry was out.

Clicking from website to website, Jason continued his quest. Perhaps he could get her something for the baby. *No*, he thought. *This is Jodie's gift.* There was plenty of time to get stuff for their baby. *Something for the house? No, not personal enough. Lingerie? That wouldn't be good.* It would still be months before they could enjoy the intimacies of a married couple. A spa day? That wasn't Jodie's style. This was the first time that Jason had ever struggled with a gift for his wife. He dropped his head to his hands and said aloud, "Oh, help me find the perfect gift." His statement turned into prayer, as he asked God to truly help him to discover what his special gift to Jodie should be. He knew that he needed to decide on something soon, as shipping could be a problem as Christmas Day approached.

For each of the landscaping crew, Jason had bought an oversized heavy-duty travel mug. Inside each, he had placed a $1000 bonus check with an extra $100 for each year that they had been working for him. For Matt, there would be an additional $1000 because of all the extra he had done since the accident. He had also gotten a travel mug for Jodie since she had truly been such an important part of the crew for the past few months. Inside her mug, he put a sweet note, outlining what she had done for the company as the bright, young assistant.

Jodie's week was busy as she mailed gifts to Jason's parents and to his sister's family. They sent a large coffee pod sampler and two beautiful large coffee mugs to his parents. There had been very few years that they hadn't heard how the gift they gave was just not quite right. The comments almost always ended with his mother's saying, "But it's the thought that counts. Thank you." His sister was nearly as bad; she had learned well from her mother. Jodie tried to erase the negative thinking from her brain.

As she left the packages at the UPS depot, she forced herself to turn the bad thoughts into prayers for them. "Help me, God, to see them the way You see them. Help me to love them from an overflowing of the love that You have shown to me." As she prayed, she was struck by how she often displayed the same lack of gratitude for all that God had done for her. She asked forgiveness and prayed that she herself would be more grateful.

For her parents, Jason and Jodie had selected a week's stay at a luxury cottage on a lake in northern Minnesota. Her dad and mom would enjoy the fishing and the hot tub that overlooked the lake. Jason was given two weeks at the cottage by one of his landscaping clients as a bonus for finishing ahead of schedule and for doing such an impressive job. They planned to use the second week next January—a year from now—as a celebration of their sixth wedding anniversary. Of course, by then, they would have a nine-month-old baby in tow. That reality was still a foreign thought.

Kristen had requested things for her baby, so Jason and Jodie bought onesies, diapers, and a stroller. They knew her parents were getting her a crib.

Beyond that, there were Jodie's grandparents on her father's side. They were always thrilled with whatever they got. Jodie often commented how she wanted to be like her own grandmothers. Jason's paternal grandparents had both passed away, and he had not had any contact with his maternal grandparents since he was four. His memory of them was very scant. There had been a falling out between his grandparents and his mother, and all communication was ended. About ten years ago, when he asked his mother about them, he was told that they had moved to somewhere in Arizona. Jodie thought that Jason and she should try to find them this next year.

Jodie had gotten new floor mats and a leather steering wheel cover for the new truck that Jason had picked out. The mats were the customized type designed to hold spills of all sorts. She knew Jason would really like them. As she wrapped his gifts, she couldn't wait for Christmas morning to see Jason's reaction when he unwrapped them.

Jodie and Kristen baked and decorated cookies to take to their neighbors. This tradition, another of Mormor Lindstrom's, had been continued by Jodie's parents and by Jodie and Jason. On the twenty-third, they would go door to door delivering the cookies. Jodie was grateful that since Jason could now navigate in a wheelchair, he would be able to participate in their tradition.

Chapter 20

With just a week left before Christmas, Jason still had not decided on a gift for his wife. Had his physical confinement confined his brain as well? Everything he thought of seemed so lame. Interesting word, wasn't it? Lame—that was just what he was—literally.

Never before had he asked for God's help in choosing a gift, but he was completely out of ideas. As he prayed, he asked for God's blessing on his wife and thanked God for her. What could he put in a box and place under the tree that would truly elate her? He knew he had to start thinking out of the box. The box—that was it! Ever since they moved into their house, they had called their unfinished basement "the box" because it lacked everything; it was like a big, empty box. He would have the basement finished. It was already plumbed for a bathroom. He could use his crew, as they were available and willing, to supply the labor. Landscaping guys could certainly do carpentry and finish work. If they could build pergolas, bridges, fountains, and gazebos, they could do framing. He knew Matt could do drywall.

Jason started sketching out the layout for a family room with a fireplace and a kid play space, a bathroom, a guest room, a storage room, and an actual laundry room with a wash tub. He had seen enough basement remodels on TV to know just how to begin. He knew that his own creativity would kick in as soon as he began his design. On Christmas morning, Jodie would unwrap a box with detailed plans, sketches, and pictures for "The Box." This would be a gift that would keep on giving for many years to come. Jason smiled as he pictured Jodie's reaction. This was going to be great!

Now that he could get himself around the house, Jason didn't need twenty-four-hour care. Jodie enjoyed her freedom to go shopping and do errands that had been postponed. Jason was grateful for the time that Jodie was away so he could work openly on his Christmas gift.

Jason and Jodie were also able to attend church again and take part in the special Christmas activities there.

Jason had found a lidded box just the right size in which he could build an actual model of the renovation. Using his artistic creativity, he began to make The Box come alive. As he placed the miniature walls, fireplace, couch, tables, chairs, a mini kitchen, and a kid area, he imagined his little family enjoying winter evenings by a cozy fire.

The sound of the garage door opening prompted Jason to hurriedly hide The Box's box into his stack of magazines, books, and work notebooks. Jodie never touched his pile of stuff, so he knew his surprise was safe there. He wheeled himself toward the door of the garage to greet his wife.

Jodie appeared with her arms laden with grocery bags. Even though she tried to remember to use those reusable bags she kept in the car, she usually forgot and ended up with more plastic bags. She rationalized the action by reminding herself that the plastic bags kept her from buying trash can liners, so they did get reused. Jason laughed aloud when he saw the bags hanging clear up to her elbows on both arms and four more bags clutched to her chest. "Is there anything I can do to help?" He chuckled as he shook his head. "I think that, even if you had thirty bags of groceries, you would get them all into the kitchen in one trip!"

"You are just jealous," Jodie responded. "You've heard of one-trick ponies? I am a one-trip lady!" She placed all the bags on the table as Jason closed the door.

"It feels really good to be able to do some things to contribute," Jason said as he put a bag of canned fruits and vegetables onto his lap and wheeled them to the pantry. "Oops, I didn't realize how high these shelves are. I guess I am not contributing as much as I thought I was."

His wife came to his aid and put the cans on the shelves as he handed them to her. "Your contribution is very much appreciated, my love. I can't believe how well you are doing."

"It will still be a long time until I am self-sufficient. I keep thinking that I am making progress all the time, and then I remember that surgery is coming, and I will lose ground. It's kind of depressing."

"I know. The surgeries will have their own setbacks, but each one will bring you closer to the end goal."

"I just wish that the projected schedule did not have a surgery so close to the due date for our baby."

"Let's wait and see how you do with this one and the one scheduled for March. Maybe we can tweak the schedule to get that May surgery moved up to April." Jodie placed her hand on Jason's shoulder.

Jason wheeled himself back to the table and started unpacking the produce. "I know I can get these put away into the refrigerator on my own. The fridge and I have become pretty good buddies. I make a point of visiting my friend several times a day."

Since Jason was continuing to do well, they decided that Jodie could return to work after Christmas. She contacted her supervisor, Robin, and told her of her plans. Robin was thrilled to have Jodie back on the schedule, telling her that things had not really changed much. It was the same old story of working short and not enough on-call nurses available to fill in. She was very understanding toward Jodie's taking more time off when Jason had his upcoming surgeries. Again, she reminded Jodie that she should take as much time as she needed.

They were just finishing putting everything away when a breathless Kristen burst through the front door. "It is really getting slick out there. I spun out trying to get up the hill on Thirty-Fourth. I am so thankful that there wasn't a car coming down the hill. We would have collided for sure."

Kristen removed her boots by the door and sat down in the La-Z-Boy. "Work was hard today! Everybody and his brother were out doing their week-before-Christmas shopping. Then I had that horrible ride home!"

"It wasn't so bad when I went grocery shopping. It was just beginning to spit snow," Jodie replied as she went to the window. "Oh! Oh my! I don't think they were predicting this!" she exclaimed as she gazed at the heavy snowfall and the quick accumulation. "Jason, look! There must be two inches already on the roads. And look at the size of those snowflakes. I hope we don't get a lot of wind and drifting with this."

As if on cue, the wind began to pick up, and the snowflakes got smaller and were whipped around in little whirlwinds. Jason peered out the window. "Looks like the crew will have some plowing work for tonight and tomorrow. I'd better start calling so they will be prepared."

Kristin checked the weather app on her phone. "It now says that we could get up to eight inches of snow out of this. I know they didn't predict anything like this when I watched the weather forecast this morning."

As Jason made his calls to his crew and got them ready to cover their clients, the sisters started dinner.

"I am so glad you are okay, Kristen," Jodie began. "We certainly don't need any more accidents this year."

"I am too," her sister replied. "You know, when the car was so out of control, it made me do some thinking. I thought that my life has been pretty much like my car. I have been traveling some rather slick roads with lots of hazards and have been kind of out of control."

Jodie stopped peeling the potato in her hand and turned toward Kristen. She didn't say anything but nodded her head.

Kristen continued, "Now, mind you, I am not ready to get all religious or anything like that, but I felt like angels or something, God maybe, was there in the car with me. It was almost like someone else took over the steering wheel and got me through the spinout."

"God does love you, Kristen, and He wants to protect you. I believe there are times that angels do intervene in our lives."

"Whatever it was, I am thankful. I don't think there was any time in my life when I felt more helpless. I thought that I could die—or my baby could die—or both of us could die. I am so glad to be home. I am not looking forward to driving to work tomorrow morning."

Jodie looked at the swirling snow through the kitchen window. "It should be better by then. The snowplows will be out all night. There may not be school, though, if it continues."

"Can you believe that in a few short years, we will be interested in the school closures?" Kristen remarked as her hand instinctively moved across her abdomen.

"No." Jodie laughed. "That does seem odd. To think we will need to make decisions about schools. Jason and I have talked a little about homeschooling our kids."

"Kids? You having twins?" Kristen teased her sister.

"No, silly, I am talking about ones that we would like to have after this one."

"Yikes! I am wondering what life will look like with one, and here you are planning a tribe."

"We all wish that your circumstances were different and that you could see this baby as truly a blessing and not a burden," Jodie said.

"Me too," Kristen replied. "It seems like much of my day is spent trying to figure out how I am ever going to afford a place of my own, how I am going to keep my old car running, how I am going to go to school, how I going to run a business, and how I am going to raise my child. It all seems so overwhelming that it wears me out just thinking about it all."

"Maybe it's time, Kristen, that you let someone else take control of the steering wheel."

"I know what you are trying to say, but I am not ready for that. I am not ruling out that I might be ready someday—just not now."

"I understand, I think," Jodie said as she turned her attention back to the potatoes and changed the subject. "I am going back to work right after Christmas. I get my schedule tomorrow."

"Is Jason okay to be on his own all day?" As soon as she asked the question, Kristen knew the answer. "Of course, he is okay. Look at him getting around."

"Yeah, Robin said that she was really glad I would be back, if only for a few weeks anyway, before Jason's surgery."

Kristen started putting the dishes on the table. It was good to have Jason at the table for meals. Thoughts of her life again filled her brain. What would it be like to have her own home, to have a caring husband like Jason, and to be setting her own table for her own family? She could almost picture the highchair holding a little blond cherub. *No, that will be Jodie's reality.* She frowned. For her, it would remain only a dream. The familiar feelings of jealousy began to creep into her heart. She knew that God really didn't owe it to her. She had chosen not to do things the way she had been taught. She was in control, wasn't she?

Chapter 21

True to the revised forecast, they got about eight inches of drifting snow during the night. Surprisingly, most of the schools were open. Jason had commented that since it was the week before Christmas, the kids probably had projects to finish and parties that could not be missed. The street in front of Jason and Jodie's house had been plowed, but their driveway had a huge drift that nearly engulfed Kristen's car.

Kristen quickly showered and dressed, thinking that she would need a lot of extra time to get her car shoveled out. As she descended the stairs, she saw Jason opening the front door. Her heart gave a little leap as she saw Matt standing there.

His eyes traveled up the stairs to meet hers. "Do you have your keys? I'll dig that buried car out for you."

"Yeah-uh, yes, thank you," Kristen stammered. "Let me get them."

Jason invited Matt into the house, but he declined, citing his snow-caked boots. He said that he would be working on the walkway until he got the keys. The sound of the snowblower gave proof of Matt's work.

What a thoughtful guy he is, Kristen thought as she slipped on her coat and boots to take the keys to Matt.

"Here are my keys. Do you want me to scrape the windows?"

"No, you go back in where it is warm and eat your breakfast. I'll be done in no time." He smiled.

Sitting at the table with Jodie and Jason, Kristen said, "That is really nice of Matt to dig my car out. I am surprised that he even thought of it since neither of you has to go anywhere this morning."

"He's a good guy," Jason responded, "especially when you think that he has already been working since two in the morning. He's just taking a little break before he gets back to our real clients. They don't come much better than Matt." Jason put down his piece of toast and wheeled to look out the front window. He noted that Matt had the sidewalk all cleared and had moved Kristen's car, freed of its coat, into the street. Using the snow blade, he was now clearing the drive and was almost finished. "Wow! He is practically done. I'll get some coffee ready to refill his old travel mug. Jodie, did I perchance see some chocolate doughnuts in the stack of groceries you bought?"

"I was going to save them for the weekend, but go ahead. I can get some more, and I know they are Matt's favorite," Jodie responded as she retrieved the doughnuts from the cupboard.

"We'll have to catch him, because if I know Matt, he will be on his way as soon as he is finished," Jason warned.

"I'll go get his cup. I have to get my keys back anyway," Kristen volunteered.

Not a moment too soon, Kristen donned her coat and boots again and went outside to get Matt's cup. Matt was driving her car back into the drive.

"I need your cup so I can give you a coffee refill," she said as he stepped from the car and handed her the keys.

Matt smiled as he jogged to the truck to retrieve his travel mug. Cup in hand, he smiled as he anticipated the fresh coffee.

"Anything in it?" Kristen asked.

"No, it's empty." Matt laughed.

"You goofball! You know what I mean. Do you want anything in your coffee?" Kristen gave him a playful punch on his arm.

Still laughing, Matt replied, "No, I like it black."

While Kristen filled his mug, Matt loaded the snowblower and shovel into the back of his truck. He still had a couple of parking lots to scrape before nine o'clock, and then he would tackle a few residential jobs.

Hiding the doughnuts behind her back, Kristen returned with his sad-looking mug.

"Thank you so much," he said as he took the cup. "Do you know what would be perfect with this coffee?"

"A warm fire maybe? Or perhaps some chocolate donuts?" Kristen asked as she pulled the doughnuts from behind her back. "Jason's idea. Jodie said they were your favorite."

"She is right. They are!" Matt eagerly took the doughnuts and pulled one from the box. "This right here makes starting work at two a.m. all worthwhile." With that, he waved to Jodie and Jason, who had been watching out the window. He thanked Kristen for the coffee and doughnuts and walked to his truck.

Kristen took a few breaths of the crisp air and hollered to him, "Thank you so much for getting my car out—and scraped!"

Matt turned back and tipped his head. "My pleasure! Drive carefully!"

As she walked to the door, she couldn't help but wonder if her future could ever include a nice guy like Matt. With the way she had messed things up, how could it? What nice guy would ever want someone who would soon give birth to another guy's kid?

The thoughts continued as she drove to work. She was, indeed, grateful for her family and the way they all had been helping her. They never said things that added to her guilty feelings, but she still struggled with that and with her old jealousy. Everything always worked out right for Jodie. Kristen made a fist and pulled her elbow toward her waist—or what used to be her waist. She would make it! She was strong! Lots of other single moms made it. Lots didn't make it or barely made it, but she would be different. She would make it all work! She was in control! Or at least she would be in control once she got her own apartment, a reliable car, an education, and her coffee shop.

Chapter 22

With Jodie around all day, Jason had difficulty finding time to work on The Box. He was relieved when his wife said that she was going to go upstairs to iron her scrubs so they would be ready for work next week. Jason told her that he needed some time to work on a Christmas present and asked that she let him know when she was done so the surprise would not be spoiled.

"Sure, I have some other things to do up there, so I will just plan on about two hours before I come back down."

Listening to Christmas music on her phone, Jodie skipped her way up the stairs. Calling back to Jason, she chirped, "I just love Christmas surprises!"

Jason finished his renovation model and closed the box. He slipped his drawings and specs into an Igland Landscaping manila envelope, which he taped to the inside of the box top. Choosing the blue snowflake paper and a huge silver bow, he wrapped his package and placed it under the tree. *She is going to love it*, he thought. He knew that he would love it too. The design was perfect. He closed his eyes and pictured their little family—Jodie, himself, and their baby—in the newly designed space. Yup—that was perfect!

Because he could now sit for four to five hours in the wheelchair, Jason suggested that Jodie and he spend some time ringing bells for the Salvation Army. Two days before Christmas, they tended the kettle and greeted shoppers at their local grocery store. Those who knew of Jason's accident were surprised and pleased to see how well he was recovering. Even though the special foam padding added comfort, the four-hour shift did get long for Jason. They were pleased with the amount of money they were able to collect for families in need. This, they decided, should become a new part of their family's Christmas traditions. They talked about how fun it would be to have their little one ringing a baby-sized bell.

Before they knew it, it was December 24. Jason and Jodie were off on their trek of delivering the Christmas gifts to the crew. Each of them was grateful for the mug—the fancy kind that didn't spill. Every one of them had to be prompted to look inside. Each was surprised at the amount of the check and freely expressed their gratitude.

"How could you afford this—with the accident and all of the medical expenses?" Phil asked.

"God provided," Jason replied. "We had a good year, despite the accident."

"I'm glad I didn't get fired, and I am glad I didn't quit. You really helped me, you know, to put everything in perspective. I've been looking at myself and my contributions to the company in a new light since our talk. It made a difference. I just want to thank you."

"You are welcome. And I want to thank you for hanging in there and giving it a second chance," Jason said as he shook Phil's hand. "Merry Christmas!"

"And a merry Christmas to you, Jason and Jodie!" Phil dropped Jason's hand and reached both arms inside the car to hug his boss. "You don't know how you helped me in changing my outlook on life."

The last stop was Matt's house, or more correctly, Matt's mother's house. Three years ago, his father died of a sudden heart attack. They had called it the widow-maker, and for them, it certainly was. The doctor explained that it got its name because it was a fatal heart attack that had no warning and occurred in younger men. Many would think it a bit odd that Matt was still living at home at age thirty, but the house was spacious, and its layout gave him his own space. He lived in the daylight basement that had been converted into a one-bedroom apartment. With his own entrance, Matt had the separation that he desired. Since the rent was considerably less than comparable apartments in the area, he had been able to save up for a down payment for a house of his own. His plan was that he would keep saving until his fiancée and he could select a house together. That would be the case, if only he had a fiancée. He thought he would have found the right woman by now, but that was not the way things had worked out.

Matt was equally amazed at the size of his gift. "I can't imagine working for anyone else."

"My greatest concern about you, Matt, is that someday you will strike out on your own and become my competition."

"I hadn't thought of doing that, but now that you mentioned it …" Matt joked.

Jason shook a finger at Matt. "Stop right there. I am sorry now that I said anything."

Matt looked again at the check in his hand. "Well, thanks a lot for the bonus! I'm not sure what I am going to do with it yet."

"I'm sure you will figure it out," Jason said. "But if you need some help, let me know."

"No, I've got this." Matt smiled. "You going to the service tonight?"

"We wouldn't miss it," Jodie interjected. "It is one of my two favorite services—Christmas candlelight and Easter sunrise."

"Okay, I'll see you there!"

Having delivered all the mugs and bonuses to the crew, the couple headed for the hospital. Jodie had made plates of fudge and divinity for the cardiology unit staff with whom she worked and for the orthopedics unit staff who had cared for Jason after the accident. Her coworkers loved the candy plate, but they were more excited to hear that Jodie would be back next week. When they stopped by Orthopedics, Jason was greeted by everyone. They were so pleased to see how he was recuperating. He told them he would be back in a few weeks for his first of several follow-up surgeries but for a much shorter stay.

Celebrating the completion of their delivery tasks, Jason and Jodie headed home. The tradition that had been established since they had been married was that, on Christmas Eve, they would grab all the presents and go to Jodie's parents' house for dinner. Then they would go to the candlelight service together. After the service, they would return to spend the night at Dale and Bonnie's house. Kristen had not been a part of the tradition, as she had been living in New York. It was good to have her back. Jodie and Jason discussed whether Kristen would decide to join the family for the candlelight service. Thus far, she had not gone to church with them, preferring to keep her distance from all things overtly spiritual.

They took advantage of the few hours before it was time to head out by resting. They were snuggling on the bed in the family room when Kristen came in the front door and walked into the room.

"Oh, I didn't mean to intrude. Should I go back out and knock?" Kristen asked as she kicked off her boots.

"No," her sister answered. "We were just resting a bit before we headed out to Mom and Dad's."

"Since I have not been around for a while, tell me, what exactly is our current family tradition?"

Jodie got up from the bed. "Well, in about a half hour, we pack up the gifts, our overnight stuff, and clothes for tomorrow and go to our parents' home. Then we have dinner; Mom usually makes soup. We play some games. We go to the candlelight service, then home again, and sleep."

"Sounds fun! I'd better get packed. Could I ride with you guys? My car has not been acting the best," Kristen asked as she headed up the stairs.

"Sure, that would be great!" Jodie answered. At least Kristen didn't say she wouldn't go to the service. Jason and Jodie gathered their things and packed them into the Subaru. They were very thankful for the temporary garage ramp that allowed Jason to travel easily from the kitchen to the car.

Just as they were finishing, Kristen appeared with her bag. "Hey, thanks for packing up my gifts too! Look at this! It looks like we are going for a week—not just one night."

"Most of the space is taken by the gifts and the wheelchair," Jason responded. "So it's not as bad, or as good, as it looks."

The early sunset made the drive to the parents' house festive as they noticed all the lighted houses and trees. The sky was clear, and the moon was full. They talked about how it reminded them of *The Visit from Saint Nick*, as the moon really did light up the snow-covered ground and give a "lustre of mid-day to objects below."

When Dale opened the door, the three were greeted by the aroma of chili. They knew right away that their dad, not mom, had been the one in the kitchen. His chili was truly award winning, having won several chili cook-offs over the years. His trophies included "People's Choice," "Best Traditional," and "Home on the Range." There was no recipe, however, since he never wrote down the ingredients, and each new batch was a bit different from any before. His chili seemed to just get better and better.

"Yum!" exclaimed Kristen as she carried her bag inside.

Bonnie came from the kitchen and directed the girls to their rooms. That wasn't necessary since they had all spent the night there just a couple of weeks ago for the St. Lucia breakfast. Her parents had offered their own room again to Jason and Jodie, but the offer was declined. This time they would be staying in Jodie's childhood room. Dale worked with them to get the gifts in and set under the tree as the timer beckoned Bonnie to remove the cornbread from the oven.

Chapter 23

The church was not at all what Kristen was expecting. The last time Kristen had attended church with her parents, they went to an impressive building that seated five hundred or more in the auditorium. She remembered that there were several services each weekend and sessions for children, so the total attendance was well over two thousand. Tonight, they pulled up in front of an old warehouse that had been converted into a church/community center. The sign in front said, "Valley Edge Center of Hope—serving the community of Crescent Valley." The community center schedule and the church schedule were both posted.

"Does your church rent this space?" Kristen asked.

"No," her dad replied. "Our church bought and renovated this old building, and we decided that we would donate use to the community."

"You could probably make some good money by renting it to groups." Kristen had turned into a business-minded woman ever since she had enrolled in classes with her aim to start her own coffee shop.

"We talked about it, but right now it is working well to let groups use our space without rent payments. It helps to give us an identity in the community."

"I remember passing this old building on the way to school when I was growing up. I always wondered why they didn't just tear it down. I guess it did have a purpose. It looks great now." Kristen felt proud that her family had been a part of the restoration of the building. "So why did you stop going to our old church?"

"We didn't leave because we were unhappy with anything there, but we felt like God was pushing us to branch out and help start this new church.

We felt a need to have a church that was more focused on helping people who didn't feel comfortable in a traditional church," Dale explained.

The interior of the building surprised Kristen even more than the improved exterior. The large foyer was more like a lounge area with groups of comfortable chairs and small tables. She noticed a table with coffee pots and cups in a corner. *This*, she thought, *could make a great location for a coffee shop.*

"I'll be right back. Save me a seat," Kristen said to Jodie. With that, she went back outside. Just as she suspected, the community center and church were using less than half of the warehouse space. Maybe she could rent some of the unused space and turn it into her coffee shop. The road had great traffic flow, and the community was already coming there for activities. At least it was something to consider.

After what she had seen so far, she was not totally surprised when she entered the main space. There were no rows of plushy padded pews. Instead, there were rows of chairs arranged in a huge semicircle around a small table at the front. Behind it was a wedge-shaped stage. It was not a high stage with a choir loft like their old church, but a low stage with some simple chairs and music stands. On one side was a small piano, while on the other was a simply decorated Christmas tree. The piano looked so small compared to the concert-style grand piano at the other church, and there was no pipe organ. If it hadn't had the back-lit cross on the wall behind the stage, one might think that this was just an ordinary meeting hall. This was not the stuffy, fidgety church that she remembered. This one just seemed more real, more genuine, and more accepting. Kristen liked it.

On the table, she saw an advent wreath. Now that was something that looked familiar. The various candles were taller or shorter depending on how many Sundays they had burned. She remembered, as a child, watching the wax from the burning tapers cascade down, making stalactite-like formations on the sides. It had seemed to her like an artist was creating new sculptures each Sunday. The four outside purple and pink candles were already lit. Kristen remembered that each had a name like love, joy, or peace. The center white one, taller and greater in diameter than the outside one, would be lit tonight. She smiled as she remembered that it was called the Christ candle.

Kristen spotted her family in the third row, and she made her way to them. She turned when someone softly called her name. There was Matt! What was he doing here? Oh, he must go to the same church. She had observed that the relationship between Jason and Matt had seemed to be more than a boss-employee relationship. She now realized that it was more of a friendship. That would explain why Matt went above and beyond, doing things like scraping out the drive and digging out her car.

"Matt!" she exclaimed. "I wasn't expecting to see you here."

"And I wasn't expecting to see you. Jason had told me that you weren't into church that much."

"Well. It's Christmas, and I do like traditions. I'd better get to my seat. It looks like they are about ready to start." As she went to the place saved for her, she wondered what else Jason had told Matt. Did he know that she was pregnant? Did he know that she had failed in New York? Did he know that she was working a temp job and was enrolled to attend community college when most people her age already had careers?

The service started with everyone singing "Joy to the World." Even though there were only about two hundred people, it sounded great. The instruments—a flute, piano, and trumpet—really added a festive sound. The center Christ candle was lit, and the pastor explained the significance of each of the candles in the wreath. A drummer and guitar player joined the musicians as everyone sang "Jingle Bells" and "O Little Town of Bethlehem."

Two men carried rocking chairs to the front and arranged them on the stage. An older couple, dressed to look even older, came to sit in the chairs. All the children were invited to come and sit on the floor in front of them. It was quite a sight to see the smaller and larger backs of the children, with their attention focused on the grandparent-looking couple. The lights were dimmed, and the couple read the Christmas story about the birth of Jesus and the shepherds coming to the stable.

There was something about that reading that stirred Kristen's heart. *This*, she thought, *is more than tradition*. Even though she had heard the reading many times, tonight it seemed different. The words weren't different, but the way she heard them was different. Was it because she, too, was carrying a child, much like Mary on her way to Bethlehem? This time, for the first time, it seemed more real. She smiled as the words were read about Mary pondering these things in her heart. That was what she was doing—pondering.

She pondered through the singing of "While Shepherds Watched Their Flocks" and "Angels We Have Heard on High."

Kristen's attention was drawn back when a man dressed as one of the magi walked stately to the front of the auditorium. He was carrying a fancy gold-embossed box. In his deep bass voice, he told the account of the magi's coming to worship Jesus. Again, the words from the Bible went deep into Kristen's heart as she thought about the gifts the magi brought. He told how his gift, gold, was a gift fitting for a king. A second magi, carrying an ornate bottle, walked to the front. This one told how his gift of frankincense was used by the priest in the worship service of God in the temple. Then a third magi strode to join the others. He said that he brought myrrh—a dried sap from a thorny tree. Myrrh was used in preparing bodies for burial. They concluded with each, in turn, bowing on one knee and making a declaration about his gift.

The first stated, "I bring gold to honor my King!"

The second remarked, "I bring frankincense to worship my God!"

The last concluded with, "I bring myrrh to receive my Sacrifice!"

It dawned on Kristen that all of this involved giving. What had she given? What had she ever given to God? For the past ten years or more, she knew that answer was nothing. She fought in her mind as she realized that God wanted something from her. No, God didn't want something from her—He wanted her.

The men rose, and together they sang, "We Three Kings." Their rich voices blended perfectly and added a depth of meaning to the words. Each of them sang a solo verse, emphasizing the gift he had brought. Kristen had never noticed that the carol had a verse for the various gifts and described Jesus as King, God, and Sacrifice. The magi returned down the aisle to the back of the church.

By the time they had sung the last note, Kristen knew she was ready. She was ready to stop running away from God. She was ready to stop blaming God for her mess-ups. She was ready to accept the grace that Jason and Jodie had talked about. She was ready to mend the broken fences with her family. She was ready to tell God that she was sorry for the years she spent defying Him. She was ready to trust God with her future. She was ready to be a mother who would raise her child to know God. She was ready. She could scarcely believe she was the same person who had been so angry, so self-consumed, so defiant, and so miserable. She wasn't even the same person who had walked into that service, one who was thinking about an economic opportunity that she could pursue. She was ready to turn over the steering wheel of her life to God—to surrender control to Him. She wanted the service to end right then because she wanted to tell her family about the decision she had just made.

The service continued with more carols, and then candles were distributed. The pastor started talking about the reason for Christmas and that Jesus came not so we could get up early and open gifts but to die so that we could have a relationship with God. He said that anyone who wanted to begin that relationship could do so that night. Kristen knew that that was exactly what she wanted to do.

The candles were lit by passing the flame from one person to the next, and then remaining lights were turned off. The soft glow of the candlelight matched the glow in Kristen's heart. As the group sang "Silent Night," she was truly feeling that all was calm and all was bright. She no longer had to figure it all out by herself. God would be in control.

Everyone blew out their candles, and the three magi again came to the front, each carrying a bag. The pastor said that they had a special treat for each person. Kristen was excited to see the brown lunch bags with twisted tops. She remembered that, in their former church, everyone would get a bag just like those. The Christmas bags always contained an apple, an orange, peanuts in the shell, and a few pieces of wrapped candy. She secretly hoped that the contents of these bags would be just that.

"Our magi will give you bags as you leave. But listen up—this year, everyone will be getting two bags," the pastor said. "One is for you, and one is for you to give away to someone who needs it. Ask God to show you that someone."

Kristen at once thought of the homeless people that used to hang out around Pete's coffee place. She was sure that they would still be there, and she knew that was where her extra bag would be going.

The pastor prayed and then shouted, "Merry Christmas!"

No sooner had he finished than Kristen grabbed Jodie's arm. "I did it!"

Jodie looked curiously at her sister and began thinking about what

Kristen might have done when she went back outside. "Did what?" she tentatively asked, grimacing and bringing her hand to her forehead.

"No, no—nothing like whatever you might be thinking. I gave the steering wheel of my life to God. I am no longer out of control. I made my decision to give Him control."

Jodie's eyes widened, and her mouth flew open. "No way! God has forgiven my past, and my future belongs to Him."

"Way!" Kristen nodded as tears began to fill her eyes. "For real!"

Jason and her parents were busy talking with other people, but Jodie interrupted them all. "Excuse me, but I think Kristen has something to tell you."

Beaming and with tears beginning to trickle down her cheek, she started, "Tonight, I turned control of my life over to God. Mom, Dad, I am so sorry for the grief I put you through, especially the last ten years."

Now the tears flowed freely. "I was so insistent on running my own life my way that I turned completely away from what I should have been doing. But tonight, everything became clear as I heard the Christmas story. It was almost as if I had never really heard it before."

"Oh, Kristen!" Her mother embraced her. "You don't know how your dad and I have prayed for this day." Tears also streamed down her cheeks.

Dale hugged his daughter. "This is the best Christmas gift ever! Let's go home and celebrate!"

"How do you celebrate this?" Kristen asked.

"I'm not sure, but I think we can find a way," her dad replied as he put on his coat.

For some reason, Kristen felt like she wanted to tell Matt, but when she looked to where he had been sitting, she didn't see him. Matt had already left. She thought it unusual that she would be disappointed in not getting to tell him about her decision, but she was. She knew that she couldn't possibly have feelings for him. He would never want someone like her.

Chapter 24

It was still early when Kristen awoke on Christmas morning. She remembered when she and Jodie were kids, how they would wake their parents at six o'clock, anxious to open their stockings and gifts. She checked her watch, and sure enough, it was six o'clock. Maybe she should go see if Jodie was awake.

Deciding against disturbing her sister, Kristen made her way to the kitchen to start some coffee. She flipped on the Christmas tree lights and settled on the couch. In the quietness of the morning, she again thought about the decision she had made the previous evening. Yeah, it was real. She felt as if her life was just beginning. She felt free. She felt light—well, maybe not literally so light. She moved her hand to her belly and could tell that she had the beginnings of a baby bump. Her baby was growing.

Just then, she thought she might have felt her baby move. She was amazed that she was so happy about it. Up until now, she had considered the baby as another reminder of her messed-up life. But even that was different this morning. Was it because she knew that God had control now? Was she beginning to see her baby not as a burden but as a gift? She wanted everyone to wake up so she could tell them about the baby.

When the coffee finished brewing, she could wait no longer.

"Wake up, sleepyheads!" she shouted down the hall. "It's Christmas, and we're burning daylight!"

"What do you mean?" Jason hollered back. "It's not daylight yet, so we can't be burning it."

"Just get coming!" Kristen replied.

In just a few minutes, the whole robed family was in the kitchen.

Bonnie got the cinnamon rolls that she had made the day before and placed them in the oven to warm. She would ice them when they were fully warmed.

"There is a reason that I couldn't let you all sleep any longer," Kristin stated.

"I know, I know, you wanted to see what Tomten had brought for you," Jodie replied.

"Well, yeah." Kristen chuckled at her sister's reference to the Swedish Father Christmas. "But there is another reason."

Pointing with both forefingers to her belly, she fairly screamed, "I think I felt my baby move!"

Jodie squealed, "That is great! I haven't felt anything yet."

Everyone got a cup of coffee and sipped until the cinnamon rolls were ready. They stood like a sentry as Bonnie squeezed copious amounts of icing onto her mouthwatering breakfast. Armed with rolls and brew, the group made their way to the living room and the tree. Packages were strewn below the tree, and there were stockings hanging from the mantel. Kristen was pleased to see her old familiar stocking there and wondered if her mother had hung it each year while she was away. Bonnie thoroughly enjoyed filling the stockings even though the kids were grown. She always included a new toothbrush, toothpaste, and floss. The rest was gum, lip gloss, and other everyday items. This year, the girls each got a bath bomb that Bonnie had made at Center of Hope community craft class, and the guys' stockings held small flashlights. Everyone enjoyed emptying the items out of their stockings, "their gifts from Tomten."

Everyone got a coffee refill and returned for the opening of the big gifts. The first one went to Bonnie from Dale. Bonnie beamed as she lifted the blown glass vase from the box. It was one that she had so admired on their vacation to an artist settlement in Wisconsin last summer. "How'd you ever get this? Did you order it and have it shipped?"

"No, I picked it up while we were there."

"But how? I was there with you. And I took everything out of the car when we got home. You carried everything inside." Bonnie was puzzled.

"Remember when I went out to fill the car with gas after we got back to the hotel?"

"Yes."

"And remember how I took the spare out of its place because I said I didn't want to have to unpack everything in case we needed it?"

"You went and bought the vase and put it in the spare tire storage area!"

"I did. And you didn't even say anything the next day when I had to get gas after we had only traveled a hundred and fifty miles." Dale walked to his wife's side.

"Oh, Dale, this is so sweet." She pulled him to herself and kissed him.

Jodie gave the floor mats to Jason, and he was thrilled. "They are designed especially for my new truck! Look how high the sides are. These will be perfect."

"I thought you would like them, sweetheart," Jodie said as she planted a kiss on the top of his head.

"I think I'd better get that truck delivered so the mats have a place to go."

"I can see it now. I have these floor mats, Mr. Truck Dealer, and I need a truck to go with them. What do you have?" Kristen teased.

Everyone laughed. It was so good to have the family united. Jodie silently thanked God for the miracle He had done to make this possible.

They continued opening gifts until the only one left was a rectangular box wrapped in blue snowflake paper. A large silver bow sat on top, along with a hand-cut angel as the name tag. Kristen picked up the box. "To the Love of My Life—My Bright Assistant," she read. She handed the package to Jodie.

Although she had seen the package previously under their own tree, Jodie was not one to snoop. She loved the surprises of Christmas morning. She twisted her head, first one way then another, as she read the stickers that adorned the package: "Do not shake. This side up. Fragile." Jason and she exchanged smiles as she began to carefully open the gift. The box inside was labeled "The Box."

"Oh, this is funny." Jodie laughed. "We call our basement 'The Box' because it is just this big rectangle with no character and nothing really inside. And Jason has now called this box 'The Box.'"

Jodie removed the tape that held the lid on the box. When she lifted the lid, she stared and caught her breath. "Oh! It is—it is The Box!" she exclaimed. "It's a model of a basement renovation. It is our basement—our box. Come, look!"

Everyone gathered around as Jodie pointed out all the features that Jason had included. She loved the fireplace and the dedicated kids' area. Bonnie saw the envelope that was taped to the inside of the lid and handed it to her daughter. Opening it, Jodie read the description and the specs of the project. It was on the familiar Igland Landscaping form, so her eyes were drawn to the expected completion date. Aloud she read, "March 15. Jason, how are we going to get this done by March 15? You have surgery coming up, and you cannot even get down there yet. And how did you get the dimensions for everything?"

"One question at a time, but they both have the same answer. Santa has his elves, and I have mine. I asked Matt to come over, and using your FaceTime technique, we got the dimensions so I could scope the project.

"And," Jason continued, "my elves, better known as my crew, are going to be working here in the basement when they don't have snow removal to do. This will help get them through the lean time, and I can assure myself, as much as possible, that they will all stick around for the next landscaping season."

"That is brilliant!" his wife responded. "Oh, Jason, this is the best Christmas gift ever!"

The two embraced and shared a kiss. "Thank you, sweetheart," Jodie whispered in his ear.

"I hate to interrupt this endearing moment," Kristen broke in, "but that is not the best Christmas gift ever. God gave the best ever. And I don't think the new basement is even the best gift this year."

Everyone turned to look at Kristen as she continued. "The best this year was actually God's gift to me last night when He helped me to realize my need of Him."

"You are so right, Kristen. My comment was very shortsighted," Jodie answered. "The gift you mentioned is by far better. I still really, really like my gift."

Having opened all the gifts, their attention turned to the dinner. Bonnie and the girls worked in the kitchen, while Dale and Jason studied the renovation model. Together, they made several mental trips to the Igland basement to fully picture the changes to be made.

The dinner was truly a feast—baked ham, mashed potatoes, ham gravy, herbed green beans, salad, and cherry cheesecake. Everyone ate their fill and a little more.

"I wish that I had my own car now," Kristen mused.

"What do you need? I can drive you," Jodie said to her sister.

"That bag that I got last night—I got to thinking about the homeless people who hang out around Pete's coffee shop. I want to give both of my bags to them."

"That's a great idea. Since your car is not working so well, I can drive. You can have my bags too," Jodie offered.

"And mine," Jason added.

Dale and Bonnie looked at each other. "And ours!" they said in unison.

Kristen clapped her hands. "That gives us ten bags—ten people we can help in a little way."

Bonnie continued, "Look at all this food left over. I think we have enough to feed another ten people. How about we make dinners for each of the people who get a bag? I have some plastic divided picnic plates, and we have plastic silverware. Let's get busy."

Dale went to retrieve the plasticware. Bonnie got the aluminum foil and plastic storage bags of assorted sizes. Jason and the girls cleared the plates from the table and set the food up for an assembly line preparation of the meals.

"We know the food won't stay warm very long, but it will still be good," Dale reported as he brought the plates.

The family chatted, and Kristen told them what she knew of the homeless people to whom they would be delivering meals and bags. They cut the cheesecake pieces a little smaller so each meal would have some. Jason went and got the candy that had been in his stocking and put some into each bag. Everyone else did the same, agreeing that, while the candy was appreciated, they probably didn't need the extra calories, and they would be welcomed by those who had so little.

The project just seemed to keep growing, as Jason and Jodie said they had extra gloves and mittens. And stocking hats—Dale said that he had a few of those. Kristen said she really didn't have much extra, but she wanted to give her gray woolen scarf, saying, "I'm not out in the weather that much. I mainly go from house to car to work."

The girls made a quick trip back to Jason and Jodie's house to get the items that they wanted to give away. In the garage, Jodie spotted their sleeping bags. "We haven't used those since we got married. I'm giving them away."

Almost giddy, the sisters returned to pick up the food plates and other items. While they were away, the others had finished up the plates.

"Can I go too?" Jason asked as the last was packed into the back of the Subaru.

"And us too?" Dale asked.

The girls laughed.

"Sure, the wheelchair doesn't need to go," Jodie said. "You back seat people will need to hold the boxes of the meal plates."

"We can do that," Bonnie replied. "You know, this could become a new family tradition. Next year, we will cook more in anticipation of giving away meals."

"I like it!" Jason said as he wheeled to the passenger door of the car. The others squeezed into the back seat, holding the meals in their laps.

The meals and bags were given to those who were camped out near the coffee shop. Kristen was somewhat afraid that seeing the old coffee place would be a painful reminder of her former life and the way Pete had treated her. Having seen how her relationship with her family had been mended and basking in her new relationship with God, she discovered that seeing the shop only reminded her of the good that had come her way.

Everyone was grateful for the home-cooked meal and the bags. In addition, the recipients were able to divide up the extra items according to their needs. It was amazing that there were just two of them who really needed sleeping bags, and the family group had just two sleeping bags to give.

Back home, they settled in to rest a few hours before the kids would head back to their home.

The relaxed picture was shattered as a scream came from Kristen in the bathroom. Jodie and Bonnie both rushed to her.

"Help! I'm bleeding!" she screamed.

"Okay, honey, we're here. We will get you to the hospital," Bonnie comforted her daughter. "Dale," she called, "can you get our car ready? We need to take Kristen to the hospital."

"I'll get our car moved out of the way," Jodie said as she went to grab her coat.

They got Kristen into the car, and she and her parents headed to Crescent Valley Memorial. Jodie and Jason followed in their Subaru.

On the way, they prayed for Kristen and her baby.

"I don't understand it. Last night, Kristen gave herself to God, and today she might lose her baby. I know that getting right with God does not mean that we will never suffer, but somehow this doesn't seem quite fair," Jodie commented to Jason.

"No, to us it doesn't make sense, but we have to trust God," Jason replied. "We don't always see the big picture."

In her parents' car, Kristen was waging her own mental battle. Why did God allow her to get pregnant only to finally begin to see the baby as a blessing, to now have that baby taken away? Was God punishing her for the years that she had been away from Him? She closed her eyes and silently talked with God. *God, I don't know how You work, and I admit that, at first, I really did not want this baby. But now I do, even though I should not have gotten pregnant. God, please keep my baby safe.*

Bonnie sensed her daughter's distress. "Kristen, this is one of those times when we don't understand everything, but we need to trust God."

"I know, Mom. I am trying to do that, but it is so hard." Her trembling voice showed the difficulty she was having.

At the hospital, Kristen was admitted to the pregnancy observation area in the birthing center. The bleeding had stopped. An ultrasound revealed that the baby appeared to be okay. Kristen and her whole family felt relieved.

"There is one other thing," the OB doctor said.

"What is it?" asked Kristen, concern showing on her face.

"Do you want to know your baby's gender?"

"Uh—yes, I think I do."

"Okay then," said the doctor, pointing to the ultrasound screen. "Look here. Here is the other thing. Your baby is a boy!"

"Wow! Whenever I thought about my baby, I assumed it would be a girl since I would be raising her by myself. I guess I am going to need to shift gears. A boy. Oh, my! I am having a little boy!"

Kristen grabbed both sides of her head as the reality of what she had just said sunk into her brain.

"A grandson," said Dale. "I guess I'd better get my fishing poles ready for our papa/grandson fishing days."

Kristen was kept for observation for a few hours and then released to two days of bed rest. It was good that Christmas was on a Friday this year because it meant that she would not miss any days of work. She had been asked to work through the thirty-first to help with year-end sales and inventory. After that, she would again be without a job.

Chapter 25

The next week passed quickly, with Jodie back at the hospital on Tuesday, Thursday, and Friday. It worked well that her schedule included New Year's Eve and New Year's Day, which allowed other staff to have those days with their families. She was quickly reminded how long the twelve-hour day was, but it felt good to be back in the familiar work schedule. Their unit was a little slow because the number of heart surgeries was less during the holidays. It was nice, she thought, to ease back into things. Her new schedule would be Monday, Tuesday, Thursday, and Friday one week and Tuesday, Thursday, and Friday the next.

Kristen did not have further pregnancy complications as she returned to her job. Since it was inventory week, her boss let her work extra hours to supplement her pay. When her supervisor handed her the final paycheck on Thursday, she wished her well. Even though this was far from being her dream job, it was a job, and Kristen was disappointed that it had ended. In a few weeks, she would begin her business administration courses at the community college. She also wanted to find some time to talk to her dad about what it might take to rent part of the warehouse building and convert it into a coffee shop.

Jason started helping more at home, even making evening meals on the days Jodie worked. His surgery was scheduled for the third Wednesday of January. It would be a regular day off for Jodie, and he was expected to be in the hospital for only one night this time.

More snow on Saturday sent the Igland crew out again to excavate their WinterCare clients. This time, the snow was only about three inches. Again, Matt cleared the Iglands' drive. He was a bit disappointed that no one was home when he came by. *Well*, he thought, *I'll be back on Monday and will see them then.*

Monday was the beginning of the basement renovation—or, as it became to be known, "The Box Reno." Jodie had already left for work when Matt, Dave, and Rich all arrived at eight. Phil was out of town, visiting his sister's family, but would be back on Wednesday.

Kristen had straightened things and had her laundry in the washer. She was pleased to see the crew, especially Matt. She tried to figure out how she could tell him about her Christmas Eve experience and the change it had made in her life. She wanted Matt as a friend, even with the knowledge that it could never be anything more.

The meeting of the crew around the dining table brought all of them up to speed. Kristen had made her near-perfect scones and served them to the group. They all raved about the taste, with Rich saying that he thought they were the best he had ever had. She was secretly glad that she had never written down the minor change she had made in Pete's scone recipe, so he wouldn't be able to reproduce them for his customers. She was sure that they would be able to tell the difference. Perhaps she could use the next few weeks to try out and perfect some recipes that she could serve in her own dream coffee shop. The crew could give her the feedback she needed if she asked them. She could have some versions served side by side and have them choose the ones they liked best. She would ask her organizationally minded sister to help her set up a plan for her testing. Her excitement built as she contemplated the possibilities.

Jason sent the crew to the basement to see the project space. While they were gone, Kristen bounced her idea off her brother-in-law.

"You mean you would feed my crew fresh baked goods for their break time and cook a hot lunch for them, and you are asking me if it would be okay?" Jason asked, a bit of sarcasm in his voice.

"Yeah. That's pretty much what I'm asking. It would help me in trying out new recipes for bakery items, soups, and sandwiches."

"I certainly have no objection, and I am quite sure that the guys will agree. You do know that there will some days that they will be out working on WinterCare projects, right?"

"I can play each day by ear," Kristen said.

"The only problem that I see, then, is the withdrawal they will experience when you start school." Jason laughed.

"Thanks, Jason," Kristen said as she turned and waltzed to the kitchen.

The crew came back upstairs, and all seemed to understand the project and how they were going to proceed. The plan of baked goods, sandwiches, and soup, as shared by Jason, was received with whoops and hollers that brought Kristen from the kitchen. They all expressed their appreciation and said that they would all contribute to her expenses for the ingredients. Kristen thanked them all for their willingness to be her guinea pigs as she planned for her own business. Gratefully, she told them that any money that they might contribute would be appreciated since she no longer had a job.

The next few hours were spent with a stream of basement items being carried up the stairs and out to be stacked in the garage. They were careful to leave plenty of room for Jodie's Subaru. For lunch, Kristin had made her own version of tuna melts and French onion soup. She also had store-bought chips, but she told the guys that she intended to get some kettle-type chips from a private supplier when she opened her own place. The lunch was crowned with her peanut butter cookies. She had placed a paper beside each plate that had the menu, a roughly drawn score chart for each item, and a place for comments. She explained that she really wanted their honest opinions, as anything less would not be of help to her. The crew ate heartily—none of them disappointed that the lunches they had packed sat outside in their trucks.

The afternoon brought the sounds of demolition and the parade of men carting the debris to the dumpster that sat next to the drive.

On one of his trips back in from debris carting, Matt was stopped by Kristen.

"Can I talk to you just a minute?" she asked.

"Uh, sure," he responded.

"After I saw you at the candlelight service and after what happened to me that night, I just felt like I wanted to tell you about it," she started.

"Okay?" Matt eyed her, questioning.

"During the service that night, it was like God was talking directly to me. I had heard the verses from the Bible before, but they had never seemed so real. After the readings from the magi, I realized that I needed to give a gift to God too. And I realized that the gift He really wanted was me." Kristen smiled as she told Matt that she gave that gift to God that night and accepted the gift of salvation that God offered to her.

Matt smiled back. "That is wonderful news! I'm glad you told me. Jason had told me that you were pretty far away from God."

"Maybe not as far as he thought. I was running away from Him, to be sure, but God had been in hot pursuit for some time." Kristen turned thoughtful. "What else did Jason tell you about me?" she asked.

"What do you mean? He said you spent some time in New York and that you worked at a coffee shop."

"There's more to it. I did go to New York, but I don't work at the coffee shop anymore. Right now, I am homeless and, thus, living here with Jason and Jodie. But, maybe most importantly, is that I am pregnant, and the baby's father wants nothing to do with either of us."

"I see," Matt responded, not exhibiting any emotion one way or another. Kristen did not ask him if he knew this information previously.

"Well, I would like to think of you as a friend, and I wanted to have my friend know what was going on in my life," Kristen concluded.

"I would be honored to be your friend, Kristen. I am also glad that you will be treating us to break and lunch each day for a while." Matt looked toward the basement door. "I'd better get back down there—hard telling what those guys may be doing without supervision."

Kristen went up to her room, glad that she had made a new friend. She anticipated having some time to plan her menus for the next two weeks.

Chapter 26

Kristen set a meeting time with her mom and dad the next evening. As she drove to her parents' place, she reviewed, in her mind, her plans for a coffee shop at the warehouse. She just wasn't sure how to approach the subject with her father. She remembered when she first thought she would be a famous fashion designer and how she had spent so much time sketching her creations. Well, that didn't work out. And then she had decided she would be a model. She dieted and exercised until she was almost to the point of being too thin. That didn't work out either. Her dreams had not worked out so well in the past. In fact, they were a bust. She glanced at her crude drawings on the passenger seat, wondering if she should take them in or not. Would she be seen as too flighty if she took them in with her? She decided she would test the waters with her idea first and then get them if needed.

Bonnie and Dale sat at the table with Kristen, their full coffee cups beckoning them all to conversation.

"What's on your mind, Kristen?" her dad asked.

"You know how I am going back to school to take business courses with the possibility of having my own coffee shop?"

"Yes."

"Well, when we went to the candlelight service, do you remember that I went back outside before it started? I saw the nice foyer area and the coffee service area, and it got me thinking. I took a look at the building and saw that half of the building wasn't being used. Do you think maybe the church would rent some of the street-side space that I could turn into a coffee shop?"

"Well," Dale answered, "so far, it has not been our practice to rent out space, but nobody has ever asked about the unused space."

"I was thinking I could maybe use the coffee shop to train people who are out of a job." Kristen continued hesitantly, "And I suppose this sounds ludicrous, but I was thinking that the back area could maybe be turned into some small apartments for people who needed a place to live—people like me."

"That sounds like an ambitious plan," remarked her mother. "You have always dreamed big."

"But this time is different," Kristin replied, feeling a bit defensive. "The modeling and fashion designing were to make me rich and famous. This is to help others. I even prayed about it and asked God to show me whether or not I should pursue this."

Dale looked intently at his daughter. "You know, I think this is different. You are considering others."

"You've been thinking this through, haven't you, sweetie." Bonnie nodded her head as she smiled at their daughter.

Kristen got up from the table. "Wait just a second. I have some drawings in my car that I want to show you." With that, she ran out the door.

Her parents eyed each other. "It is truly a miracle," Bonnie remarked, "the change in our daughter."

"It is good to see her so excited about doing something positive," Dale agreed. "I hope she will not be overly disappointed if the church does not approve of her plan."

"Brrr!" Kristen exclaimed as she popped back in the door. "Maybe I should have grabbed my coat." She laid her drawings out on the table. The coffee shop and tables were sketched out, and the apartments, though small, looked adequate for one person—or for a person with a child. "You see, this side of the warehouse is where the loading dock was, and each bay could be the front of an apartment and have a door, and each apartment would be two stories. If we enclosed the big opening and added a door and a window or two, each apartment could stretch back the way row houses in New York do. That way, we could have a tangible ministry to those in need of temporary housing. By we, I mean Valley Edge, of course."

"Who are you, and what have you done with Kristen?" her dad asked kiddingly. "The old Kristen didn't seem to care too much for those who were down and out. And she would never use the word ministry or include herself in a *we* in reference to a church group."

"I think part of me changed when I found myself without a job and without a home. I realized that, without my family, I would have nowhere to stay. Then the rest of me changed when God revolutionized my whole life on Christmas Eve."

"I must say," her dad continued, "I personally like your ideas. Since I am sure that there are lots of permits and inspections involved in businesses and apartments, we would need to get someone knowledgeable to find out about those. We would need to have an architect and someone to price things out. I don't know, but there might be some special considerations or breaks for charity housing."

"Do you know anyone who can help with those details?"

"I think I might know some. There is an architect in our old church, and he might be willing to work with us. Hopefully, his price would be what we can afford, which right now is nothing," Dale said. "I am sure he would know some others with the knowledge we would need."

"I'm excited about this!" Kristen exclaimed.

"I can tell you are, honey," her mother encouraged. "Let's make a prayer contract that each of us will pray about this every day for the next couple of weeks, and we will see how God will direct."

"I like that idea." Dale nodded to his wife. "We will plan to meet again in two weeks, and I will check with my architect friend and ask about the feasibility of all of this. Let's start day one of our contract right now and pray together about this plan."

Kristen practically skipped her way to her car. She was going to have a business. Well, maybe. She knew she still faced a lot of hurdles. For one, she was still going to have a baby. And she was starting classes in a few days—she was never a big fan of school and homework. How was she going to have the study skills to make it through school?

Light rain started to fall as she neared Jason and Jodie's house. When she signaled her turn, a small puff of smoke drifted up from the steering column. "What was that?" she asked aloud as she turned off the blinker. Another thing that was wrong with her car. It had been dying at intersections sometimes, but she had always gotten it to start. And now this. She was going to have to use some of the money she was saving for an apartment to get her car fixed. She was amazed at how fast her jubilant mood turned to frustration.

Relief spread over her when she parked the car in the drive. She grabbed her things and dashed to the door. Jason and Jodie were watching TV in the family room. She told them about the plans she had and how their dad was going to talk with an architect.

"And I talked with Mom and Dad about moving home until I could get a place of my own," Kristen said. "I'll be moving out before I start school."

"Well, you know you are welcome here," Jodie replied.

"I know, but when I moved in, we agreed that it would be a short time, and I think I have already pushed the time limit of *short*."

"I have certainly appreciated your being here with Jason when I had to go somewhere."

"Thanks!" Kristen said. "But Jason doesn't need someone with him all the time now. And the crew is here much of the time most days."

"That's right," Jason interjected. "But the guys are going to miss your bakery stuff for breaks and the sandwiches and soups for lunch."

"I think I could still probably bring some by occasionally. I will have more recipes to try out." Kristen grinned. In the back of her mind, she was thinking that she would miss seeing the crew as well. In particular, there was one crew member she would miss—the one with the sky-blue eyes. She definitely would have to think up some new recipes to try.

Chapter 27

The next week went quickly, with Jodie working and Jason anticipating his upcoming surgery. The crew was making good progress on the renovation. Kristen was able to get her car fixed. She felt good that she had the money to pay for it herself. She had moved into her old room at her parents' house. She was hoping that she would be able to find another job soon so she could afford her own apartment. She set a personal goal of being out of her parents' house by the first of April. "I think I have spent too much time with Jodie." She laughed. "Here I am with personal goals and spreadsheets."

Jason's surgery went well, and he spent just one night in the hospital. Jodie was off work for three days, and then it was back to their routine.

Before her first class on Monday morning, Kristen brought cinnamon apple scones for the crew. She knew she had an underlying motive of perhaps getting some encouragement for facing the classroom. She was pleased but not surprised to see the trucks of the crew members in front of the house.

She set the scones on the table and went to the kitchen to assure that there was plenty of coffee. From the top of the basement stairs, she hollered, "Fresh scones!"

Her announcement was met with whoops and the sounds of four men scampering up the steps.

"You don't have to call us twice," Phil remarked as he topped the stairs.

"We are really going to miss this," Dave added.

Kristen smiled and thanked them.

"Oh, no. Thank you," Rich said. Rich was the quiet one on the crew. Kristen noted that he wore a wedding band.

Kristen glanced at Matt, who had not said anything yet. He turned to Jason and started talking about something in the basement project.

Kristen told them that she had to leave, and they all, Matt included, thanked her and wished her well with her classes.

On the way to the college, Kristen thought about her past relationships with men. Now that she had given control of her life to God, she felt ashamed of her past. She wasn't quite sure how to move forward. Would she ever be able to have another relationship? How would it be different? She thought about Jodie and Jason. Could she ever have a relationship like they had? Well, that was not something for now. She was a student, a mother-to-be, and a potential business owner. That was enough. She certainly didn't need to complicate things any further.

Kristen downloaded the syllabus of her first class, Accounting 101. As she scrutinized the course requirements, she thought she could manage the assignments. Her professor was exactly how she pictured an accountant. He was monotone and completely nonanimated. She was glad she had this class first period on Mondays, as she wasn't sure she could stay awake had it been later in the day.

Her second class, Entrepreneurship 103, was after lunch. This was the class about which she was most excited. This one, she felt, would give her the tools to begin her own coffee shop. She took a seat near the front and opened her laptop. The classroom looked like it could accommodate thirty to forty students, and it began to fill. She was surprised that there were so many people interested in beginning their own businesses. Kristen looked around the room and noted that there were quite a few older students in the class.

A young man took the seat next to her. He introduced himself as Paul Winters, and Kristen couldn't help but notice his handsome face. She stole a peek at his hand and did not see a ring. *That is good*, she thought. No sooner had that thought entered her brain than she shook it out. *Remember, Kristen*, she told herself, *you are not interested in a relationship.*

This professor was the antithesis of her first instructor. She was young, energetic, and very much an extrovert. She would be the perfect one to start a business—optimism and confidence exuded from every part of her. She was dressed in a smart suit, and her hair and makeup were done perfectly. Kristen looked down at her jeans and sweater and did a mental comparison. *Not even close*, she thought. *Is that what it takes to be an entrepreneur?*

The professor, Ms. Cassandra Halverson, took command of the class with her first words. She told of her past business accomplishments and why she was teaching this class. It was the only class that she, as an adjunct professor, would be teaching. She wanted to help others who wanted to succeed in starting their own businesses. "It is my way of giving back," she said.

Kristen was absolutely captivated as she listened to this young woman who was so successful. Her business prowess was inspiring. When she mentioned that some students who were working on their master's in business administration (MBA) at the nearby state university were looking for some new start-up businesses with which they could work to fulfill a project requirement, Kristen came to full attention. She would love to have someone collaborate with her on business plans. At the close of the class, she hurried to be first in line to sign up for a student team to help her with her plan. She took the project sheet, where she would outline her dreams for her coffee shop. When she turned around, she was surprised to see that there was not a big line behind her. In fact, she was the only one from the class who was there to sign up. All the others had left the classroom. The sheet was due next week, but Kristen made her way to the student union to complete it right away. Remembering something that Jodie had told her concerning her own college experiences, she used her phone to take pictures of the application before she placed it in the professor's inbox in the adjunct staff lounge area. She couldn't wait to get home and share her unexpected possibility with her parents.

Where did that come from? she wondered. Since when did she start getting excited about sharing anything about her plans with her parents? Kristen shook her head and smiled at the change that was taking place within her. She was thinking that she might be starting to like the new Kristen. It was nice having restored connections with her family.

She decided, since she would be arriving home before either of her parents, she would make one of the new soup recipes she had recently found. She stopped at the superstore on her way home and picked up all the fresh ingredients that she would need for her basil-tomato chunky soup. She also grabbed some fresh-baked sourdough bread and three kinds of cheese so she could make gourmet grilled cheese sandwiches. Soup and sandwiches were always a tasty combination on a snowy winter night. She decided that, in her own shop, she would have a signature soup that she would make every day, a daily special soup that would be served on a particular day of the week, and a chef's choice soup that would change every day. She wasn't sure yet which soup would become her signature, but she would try them out on her family and the guys on Jason's crew.

Chapter 28

The snow continued throughout the night. Jason's WinterCare crew guys had a 2:00 a.m. start on their rounds of businesses. With the rate the snow was falling, they soon realized that they were fighting a losing battle. By 5:00 a.m., snow levels had reached nearly twenty-four inches, and the area schools were giving notice of a snow day. Matt smiled as he remembered how, as a boy, he would wake up early to watch the school closures on the television. On a normal school day, it was hard to get out of bed in time to get dressed and have breakfast before the bus came. But when there was a chance or even the slightest possibility of a snow day, he couldn't stay in bed. When he would hear or see his school's name, he would holler and jump around the house until the entire family was awake. He now imagined a new generation of young boys waking their families at an ungodly hour.

Since the snow continued to fall, he called the others on the crew who were out and suggested that they finish their rounds and then go back and start over. It would be a long day. Matt then called Jason to see if Jodie could use a lift to work. He knew she would not enjoy driving in this weather, and he was sure the hospital could use her help. Jason, as always, was grateful for Matt's thoughtfulness, and Jodie readily accepted his offer.

Jodie was ready when Matt arrived and greeted him with fresh hot coffee and a couple of big chocolate doughnuts. She had also packed a small bag for herself, just in case she had to stay over at the hospital. Matt told her to let him know if that happened, and he would go spend the night with Jason.

"How'd Jason ever get such a great crew member and friend as you?" Jodie asked as she took another sip of her own coffee.

"I'm not sure how to answer that. I think I might be the lucky one," he replied. "There are not very many guys who get to work at what they really enjoy and get to work for and with their best friend."

The traffic was not nearly as heavy as usual because the schools were closed. It appeared that many people were taking to heart the aired traffic warnings and were avoiding going out. Matt was thankful for his heavy truck with the blade, which he used as he traveled the side roads. Once they got on the freeway, they were able to take advantage of the lanes that had been somewhat cleared by the big county and city snowplows. Even here, the snow was still trying to win the battle.

"So how's your sister doing?" Matt queried.

"You probably know about as much as I do. She started school, and for the most part, she seems to like her classes. Kristen was never a bookworm, so it seems strange that she has gone back to school voluntarily."

"I think the fact that she wants to start her own business has spurred her to learn as much as she can," Matt commented as he concentrated on the partially snow-packed freeway.

Jodie chuckled. "Yes, I don't know if I have ever seen her so energized about anything. I don't think that she was even this enthused about going to New York to be a model or designer."

"Yeah, that was a challenging time on your family. I remember Jason telling me about that. The change in her in the last few weeks has been quite amazing," Matt replied.

"I think she realizes that she still faces some major hurdles," Jodie said, "but I truly believe that she is trying to trust God to work things out."

"She told me about her pregnancy the other day."

"She did?" Jodie asked, surprised that she had confided that to Matt. "Did she tell the whole crew?"

"No, just me. She told me that she wanted to consider me a friend. She also told me about the decision she made on Christmas Eve." Matt signaled for the hospital exit. "I would like to help her along, as much as I can, in the first steps of her new spiritual life."

"If you ask me, I don't think she is interested in first steps. It seems that she wants to sprint!" Jodie laughed as she thought about the way her sister could not get enough of wanting to live the way of Jesus. "She really wants to live a different lifestyle and give of herself to help others."

"Give me a call about twenty minutes before you get off, and I will pick you up."

"Thanks again, Matt. I will call you either way—if I am getting off or needing to stay. You are a good friend!" With that, Jodie hopped down from the truck and made her way into the hospital.

The night staff was thrilled to see Jodie. She was the first of her shift to arrive in their department. There was a lot of chatter about who might not make it in and who would make every effort to get there. Jodie started rounds and got updates on the patients for whom she would be caring. One patient in particular, Gary Brown, was not responding well to treatment. He was seventy-seven years old and had had a discouraging night. Jodie had cared for him several days in the past week. His wife and son, Jim, had spent the night with him, afraid that he might pass away if they left. Jodie could tell that they were really spent. After she was briefed on her other patients, she whispered a quick prayer that she would be able to offer real help to Gary and his family, and she went back to his room. Since Gary was sleeping, she took some time to talk with his family. Jodie answered their questions and assured them of the care Gary was getting. She offered them some coffee and breakfast. She asked them what else she could do to help them.

"Everyone has been so nice," his wife said. "We don't want to be a bother."

Jodie reiterated that anything that could ease their minds and make them more comfortable was no bother at all. She told them to not to hesitate to ask for anything.

No sooner had she turned down the hall than she heard a voice call her name. Looking back, she saw Gary's son.

"Can I talk to you a minute?" he asked.

Jodie could see the concern in his eyes. "Certainly." Sensing that Jim wanted to talk about something away from his mother's presence, she suggested that they go to the family room at the end of the hall. Once seated, Jodie asked, "What is on your mind?"

"I'm sure you are thinking that I am worried about my dad's heart," he began, "and I am. But what I want to talk to you about is my own heart."

"What your dad has is not contagious, so you don't have to worry about that any more than other men your age," Jodie responded. "His condition is not hereditary either—it is not inherited. So you just need to eat right, exercise, get enough sleep, and try to avoid excessive stress."

"I know all of that," Jim said.

"What is it then?"

"I have watched you as you have cared for my dad this past week, and I can tell that you are a Christian. I had a friend in high school who was a Christian. He tried to tell me about heaven and hell, and I just didn't have time for that back then." Jim took a breath and continued, "Last night, as I was thinking that Dad might die, I went down to the chapel. I wasn't sure what to do after I got there, but I lit a candle that was on the table, and I prayed. At least I think I prayed. I asked God to let my father live. I got a strange feeling in my chest, and I put my hand over my heart. I felt like my life was empty—like there was nothing real in my heart. I had always thought my life was pretty good, but I knew right then that I needed God. I asked God, that if He was really there, to have you come to work today and that you would be Dad's nurse. And, well, you did, and you are."

Jodie placed her hand on his arm. "I'm glad I'm here. How can I help you now?"

"I—I need to know how to become a Christian," he sputtered. "I should have listened better when my buddy tried to tell me way back when. I know there is some special formula, a special prayer that I need to say."

"Jim, there is not a special formula, nor a special prayer." Jodie smiled. "God knows your heart. He knows each of us. He desires to have a relationship with us. But because we are all sinners, we cannot have that relationship. It is like this: we owed God the price for our sin, but there is no way we could pay that price. God sent His Son, Jesus, to pay the debt for our sin. He died in our place to pay the price of our sin. When we accept that payment, we are spiritually born into God's family. We then have a Father-child relationship with Him."

"That's what I want. I love my dad, and I don't want to lose him yet, but I really need to have this Father-child relationship with God." With earnestness in his voice and eyes, Jim said, "How do I go about accepting that payment that Jesus paid for me?"

"That is where prayer comes in, but not a certain special prayer. Prayer is just talking to God and telling Him what is on your heart and mind." Jodie pulled out her phone and opened her Bible app to John 1:12. Reading the verse aloud, she said, "Here, in the Bible, it says that as many as received Him—that's Jesus—to them God gave the power to become sons of God."

"Thank you, Jodie. Can you stay here with me while I pray?"

Jodie nodded and listened as Jim opened his heart to the love of God and asked to be made a part of God's family.

"I know you must get back to work, and I need to get back to my family. Thank you again."

"I consider it a privilege to be involved in the healing of hearts— whether they are the physical ones or the spiritual ones," Jodie replied as she brushed a tear from her eye. "I'll be back to check on your dad in about a half hour or so. I have to make certain that my other patients are doing okay."

Jodie wished she could call Jason to let him know what had just happened, but she had work to do, and she decided that it would be better if she could tell him in person. Her shift had just started, but it could not be over fast enough for her.

During the morning, there appeared to be a modest improvement in Gary's condition. He was able to be propped up a bit in the bed for a while. He took some broth and tea. His oxygen saturation showed improvement, and his color looked some better as well. When Jodie returned to his room after lunch, she was amazed to see him sitting up and talking with his family.

"Wow! Look at you!" she exclaimed. "How long have you been up?"

"About thirty minutes," he replied.

"Let me get your temp here," she said as she slipped the thermometer under his tongue. She looked at the monitors above his bed and noted that his oxygen saturation was good. "I'm going to turn down your oxygen a bit and see how you do at a lower level."

Gary smiled and nodded.

Jodie removed the thermometer. "No fever—that's good. You look so much better than you did this morning. It's absolutely amazing!"

"I think it is God!" said Jim. "I told my parents about my experience in the chapel last night and about the conversation I had with you this morning. I told them how I now had a new Dad, which in no way lessens the importance of my old dad." He smiled and nodded toward his father.

Jodie smiled. She thought, *Here is Jim, who has known God only a few hours and is already telling other people about his new life.*

"And," Gary's wife said, "both Gary and I prayed like Jim did to become children of God too."

"That's so wonderful!" Jodie replied.

Gary turned to Jodie. "Thank you. I know now that no matter what this old heart in my body does, my spiritual heart is good and healthy."

Jodie couldn't help but think that this had to be the best day she had ever worked. Three people had been born into God's family right before her eyes.

Even though the rest of her shift was busy, Jodie nearly floated through her work. At her afternoon break time, she called Matt to tell him that she would need a ride home because all staff scheduled for the next shift had reported that they would be able to make it to work. Jodie was so pleased that she would not have to spend the night and that she could get home to share her incredible day with Jason.

Chapter 29

Jodie flew through the door and shouted out to Jason. She bubbled out the story of her day at work, and her husband grabbed her in delight as she told of Gary's family. Together they celebrated what God had done to change three lives.

"Mm—what do I smell?" Jodie asked as she wiggled her nose.

"Well, since the crew was out all day and I had nobody here, I decided that I should make us some chili."

"It smells delicious—just the perfect dish for a snowy day," she said.

"Come. It probably isn't as good as your dad's, but I think it tastes pretty good," Jason said as he turned toward the kitchen. "I even baked up some of those crescent rolls to go with it. Everything is ready."

Everything was truly ready. Jason had set the table with snowflake-patterned placemats and had a platter full of rolls.

"I am very impressed," Jodie remarked. "I didn't know that you knew where to find placemats."

"I had to hunt a while, but I found them."

"Here—you sit while I serve it up. I think it will be a lot easier for me to do it rather than your wheeling around with hot chili."

The couple savored the chili and rolls as they discussed the plans for the next few days. Physical therapy for Jason would begin again, but this time he would need to travel to the clinic. He also wanted to pick up the new truck this week. He had decided to have the Igland Landscaping name and logo painted on the doors and tailgate, rather than using their old magnetic signs. He had already worked with a sign company to finalize the design, and they had booked a time for Friday. It would be great to have a truck again, even if he, himself, could not drive it for several more months. Jason said he would take care of finalizing the arrangements for Friday morning: Jodie and he would pick up Matt or Kristen and take them to the truck dealership. Their driver would drive the Subaru from the dealership to A-1 Signs. Jodie would drive the new truck, with Jason as a passenger. Even though they agreed that it would be easier if Jason remained in the Subaru, he just had to ride in the truck for that inaugural trip. They would leave the truck at the sign company and then drop off their driver. The signs were scheduled to be completed by Friday evening. They would then find whoever was available to be an extra driver, go back to A-1 Signs, and Jodie would drive the new Igland Landscaping truck home.

Chapter 30

Both sisters were now showing their pregnancies, outgrowing their jeans and their tighter shirts. Jodie needed some bigger scrubs to accommodate her expanding frame. She invited Kristen to go shopping with her on Saturday. She couldn't remember the last time that they had shopped together. Knowing her financial situation, Kristen was relieved to hear that Jodie wanted to check out a maternity and baby resale store before they went to any department or boutique stores.

Matt was the one who was available to help in getting the truck to the sign company and then back home. The new red Ram 350, sporting the Igland Landscaping logo, fairly glistened in the sunlight.

"Hey, buddy," Jason said to Matt after both vehicles were parked in the garage, "would you do one more favor?"

"Sure—you name it," Matt replied.

"Someone very special gave me a wonderful set of custom-made floor mats that need to be put into this red machine."

"Oh, yes!" Jodie interjected. "I'll run get them." In just a few moments, she reappeared with the mats.

"Here, Matt. Have some mats!" Jodie laughed.

"Cute!" said Matt as he took the mats and put them into their right places. "I really like the space here in the back seat."

"Yep, big enough for a couple of car seats," Jason responded. "Jodie, those mats look really good in here. Thank you again!"

"You're welcome!" Jodie said as she planted a kiss on his cheek.

"Now, when we go out to do bids, we'll look very professional." Jason ran his hand over the glossy red surface of the truck. "This is nice. I can't wait until I am able to drive it."

"It won't be long." Jodie smiled.

"The doctor said I should be on crutches in another two weeks. And he said I should be able to drive in another month."

"Considering what you went through, you have done remarkably well. It will be good to see you out and about on your own." Matt looked at his watch. "I've got to get going soon, but could I get a cup of coffee before I leave?"

Jason and Jodie both laughed.

"Matt, you are welcome to a cup of coffee at our house any time you want." Jodie motioned to the door. "And I think there just might be a few of your favorite doughnuts left."

"These are still my favorite doughnuts, but I must admit those scones that your sister made beat out store-bought doughnuts. Hands down, hers are better!" Matt dunked a chocolate doughnut into his coffee and chomped down his coffee-soaked treat.

The three sat around the table, discussing the crew, the snows, and The Box.

"We should be done with the Box Reno in another two weeks if the weather cooperates," Matt announced.

"You don't know how tempted I have been to sneak down and take a peek." Jodie laughed.

"But I know you wouldn't. You gave me your word, and I trust you," her husband reminded her. "When it is done, we will have a grand reveal. You know, two weeks is perfect timing—I will be on crutches then, and I will be able to get down there too."

"I like that. Let's plan a reveal on the first day that you can navigate sans wheelchair." Jodie's planning gear kicked in. "And let's have a big celebration with Mom, Dad, Kristen, the whole crew, and their families. I'll get a big cake, and I'll ask Kristen if she will make some soups."

"Okay, the details are in good hands," Matt responded as he motioned toward Jodie. "All I need to do is get it finished.

"You know, Matt, I've been doing some thinking." Jason finished swallowing his chocolate-covered doughnut. "This remodel has gone so well that I was considering expanding the company with a remodeling business."

"Igland Landscaping, Igland WinterCare, and Igland Renovation?" Jodie asked.

"Not exactly. I want to keep Igland Landscaping and Igland WinterCare. I was actually thinking of another parallel company—with Matt being a full partner in that one." He turned to see Matt's surprised expression. "You have done such a fantastic job at directing this remodel and keeping it moving and on budget. And as I mentioned before, one of my greatest fears is that you would take off on your own and become my competition. This way, I figure that I can keep you by roping you into a partnership."

Matt shook his head in disbelief. "You know I would never compete with you. I really like working for you."

"How about working *with* me—in a partnership in the new company?" Jason questioned. "I don't want you to give an answer right now. I want you to take a month or so to think it over."

"Yeah, I'll need that time. This is huge. I will pray about it," he replied. "It has been really good to have the Box Reno job for the crew during our slow time." He glanced at his watch again. "I've got to get going. Thanks for the coffee, the doughnuts, and for the partnership idea."

On the way home, Matt replayed Jason's offer in his mind. What would a partnership mean? He liked working for Jason. How would working with him as a partner change that? His thoughts moved on to his personal future. How much longer should he live with his mother? Should he look for a place of his own? He always thought he would wait until he was engaged to buy a house and have his to-be wife help in the selection. He wanted to get married and have a family. While he had several female friends, there just had not been anyone who he considered to have marriage potential. He had kept himself so busy with his work that he hadn't given thought or effort to finding a wife. Maybe he should try one of those online dating services. They were supposed to match you according to your personality, your interests, and your faith. He had heard that it had worked out well for some people. No, that wasn't for him—at least not yet. He would trust God to bring the right woman at the right time.

Matt was paying rent to his mother and helped around the

house—mowing and lawn care, cleaning the gutters, painting, fixing things—and he did enjoy his mother's company. His mom, while devastated at the time of her husband's death, had gotten involved in a grief organization and was now leading several groups. Matt was proud of her and the way she was helping others in the same way she had been helped. Would she ever remarry? She was young enough, as if that was really a factor. She was smart and a good communicator. She had a respectable job as an office manager for a dental practice. But did she get lonely? Were the nights long? She had never mentioned any desire for another husband. She, he thought, had probably come to the same conclusion that he had—that she would meet the right man at the right time if it was meant to be. She would not say that she was trusting God, like Matt did, because faith did not play a significant role in her life. She had often expressed that she was living a good life, being kind to her fellow man, giving to charities, and not engaging in many of the vices that other people did. She was very self-sufficient. She was a good person—Matt just wished that she could share in the faith he had.

He parked his green truck on the cement slab beside the garage and walked around back to enter his home. He could smell the dinner his mother was preparing. After cleaning up, he ascended the stairs that connected his space to the main level.

He knocked on the door at the top and waited for his mother's voice to welcome him. They had installed doors at both the top and bottom of the stair and had agreed that they would always knock before entering each other's realm.

"Oh, good—you're home!" his mother called. "Come in and have some chicken stir-fry. I think I made too much. How was your day?"

"Good, good," he responded. He weighed whether or not to tell her about Jason's offer. No, he would wait—at least until he worked through the details. "We got Jason's new truck home, and it is very nice."

"They have been through a lot—with the accident and having Jodie's sister living with them."

"Oh, Kristen has moved back home with their parents, and she has started school."

"That's good. I hope she can get her life back together. It seems like she has been a bit of a lost soul."

"I think she is doing that. She is wanting to start her own coffee shop and café. She has been trying out soup, sandwich, and bakery items on us while we work on Jason's basement."

"I bet you guys aren't complaining at all about that." His mother laughed.

"You know me. Never turn down a meal or snack," Matt replied as he rubbed his belly.

"Is she pretty?"

"Huh?" Matt's head snapped up, and his eyes met those of his mother.

"Is she pretty?"

"Yeah, I guess so. She's Jodie's sister, and good looks run in that family." Matt smiled.

"Why don't you ask her out?" his mother pressed.

"I don't know—not right now anyway," he responded. He didn't want to tell his mother yet about Kristen's pregnancy and how that would severely complicate any relationship. "I'm leaving that in God's hands right now."

"Well, sometimes you might need to help God's hands along. Don't expect Him, one day, to just pop the woman of your dreams into your truck."

They both laughed.

"Since you have been redoing Jason's basement, I got to thinking that you might be able to help me with a remodeling project of my own," Jason's mother remarked as she brought a Bundt cake from the counter. "Cake?"

"Absolutely!" Jason said as he put his dishes into the dishwasher and returned to the table. "Now, what kind of remodel project do you have in mind?"

"You are looking at it. It's right here—the kitchen," she said as she waved her hand across the kitchen like she was a presenting celebrity. "It really needs to be updated. Your dad and I had talked about this before he died. We even had a designer at the House and Garden Megastore help us plan it all out."

Matt looked around the kitchen. It was rather odd that he had never noticed that the room needed some updating and redesigning. To him, it was just home—and kitchen—the place where good things were made and where friends gathered.

His mother placed the designer's plans on the table.

"Before I look at the plans, can I work on putting together what I would design?"

"You?" His mother looked at him in surprise. "Are you now a designer as well as a landscaper and a snow plower?"

"Well, maybe," he replied. "I'd just like to see what I can do. If I don't come up with something you like better, I will follow your designer's plan."

"That sounds fine." His mother shook her head and giggled.

"Let me go get a pad and tape measure so I can get the information that I will need."

"Just a minute." Carol stopped her son and started leafing through the designer plans. I have something here that I think you could use—the layout of the kitchen in its current state, with all the dimensions and measurements."

"Yeah, that will give me a head start." He marveled at the coincidence that Jason just talked to him about being a partner for a home-remodeling business, and now, less than two hours later, he was being given an opportunity to test his wings.

He asked his mother what she would like to have done. She explained that she wanted to open the kitchen up to the family room, and she wanted an island. New appliances, including a double oven, were a must, as well as modern lighting to replace the overhead fluorescent fixture that belonged in the seventies. If possible, she would like to have a walk-in pantry that had outlets and a sizable counter for baking. She did mention that his dad and she had talked about building the pantry into the front of the oversized garage since there was plenty of room in front of where the cars parked.

"Careful—just tell me what you want, not how to do it. I want to see if my brain is creative enough to do this."

"Message received," she responded, giving a quick nod of her head.

Matt looked over her wish list and asked if she wanted a special space for a single-cup coffee brewer.

"I hadn't thought of that, but that would be nice. A little coffee area would be great for entertaining."

"And had you given any thought to bumping this wall out to create a breakfast nook?"

"I hadn't. You are good," his mother remarked. "You're coming up with things that our designer didn't."

"Maybe it's because I lived here, and I know some of the problems and can see the potential." Matt surveyed the kitchen. "Yeah, I think I can design something really nice."

"Well, Mr. Designer, when might I expect to see my drawings?"

"I always ask my clients to give me a week." Matt laughed. "Will that fit into your timetable?"

His mother gave him a hug. "You certainly sound like you know what you are doing. You have so much talent. Who knows? Maybe this will open up a whole new business for you."

"Maybe," Jason responded as he picked up his notes and the layout. "I guess I'd better go and get started on this."

"You know, you don't have to do all of that right now. You do live here, you know," his mother commented.

"I know, but I do have a deadline to meet, and I really do want to get started on this." The excitement he felt inside was obvious in his voice.

He thanked his mother for both the meal and the project before he retreated down to his own domain.

Chapter 31

K risten continued to endure her accounting professor while being absolutely mesmerized by the vivacious entrepreneurship prof. She knew she needed to master the accounting because her future business would be dependent on maintaining good records and being able to handle the financial end. Operating a coffee shop was much more labor intensive than merely working at a coffee shop.

Paul always chose the seat next to hers. He was taller than she had first noticed, and his slender yet muscular build reminded her of some of the male models in New York. He could be a model, she mused—with those looks, that hair, his physique, and the confident way he carried himself.

Kristen asked him why he was taking this class.

"I have started a business of my own, and I need to get some formal training before I mess it up," he replied.

"What is your business?" Kristen inquired.

"I repair and customize fishing boats." He smiled with pride.

"What kind of fishing boats?" she asked.

"Oh, the kind that men with a more money than they know what to do with want. They are mainly bass boats under twenty feet." Paul gestured with his hands to indicate size. "These guys take their boats out on the lakes, and each wants to one-up the others. That means good business for me. I have even customized a small party barge to be used for larger fishing parties."

"Sounds interesting," Kristen quickly responded, then turned her attention to the front of the room as the professor took her place.

When the hour ended, Paul turned to Kristen and asked, "Say, would you like to meet me for drinks, and we can discuss more of our business plans?"

"Uh, yeah, I guess so …" Kristen's voice trailed off.

"Kristen?"

Kristen turned to see Ms. Halvorson standing next to her. Her professor smiled and said, "I need to talk to you a few minutes about your plan submission."

Paul looked at her. "Did you submit a plan for the MBA class?"

Kristen nodded and turned back to her professor. "Sure, I have some time right now."

Paul gathered his things and left the room.

"Kristen," her professor began, "your business plan submission was quite professional. I am pleased to tell you that one of the MBA teams selected your plan as one with which they would like to work."

"Wow! I can't believe it!" Kristen took a deep breath and looked up at the ceiling. Inhaling deeply, she asked, "What do I do next?"

"Here is the contract from the team. It outlines what they will expect from you and what you can expect from them. It includes the time commitments that will be required." Her professor handed her the multipage document.

Kristen's eyes skimmed the many paragraphs and the calendar of meetings and deadlines.

"Now," Ms. Halvorson continued, "your next step is to read through the contract. Then you need to bring it back tomorrow—signed, that is if you want to proceed."

Kristen clutched the document to her chest. "Oh, I do! I will have it back tomorrow!"

"Read it carefully so you know for sure what you are getting yourself into."

"I will!" Kristen replied. She gathered her laptop and backpack. "Thanks so much!"

Her professor smiled at her young protégé. "You remind me of someone else I know very well."

When she exited the classroom, Kristen saw Paul waiting for her.

"There you are! Now how about those drinks?" He sidled up to Kristen.

"Oh, Paul, I can't." Kristen looked at him, "You see, I was selected for the MBA project. I need to get home, go over this contract, and get ready to realize my dream."

"Okay, next time."

"Yeah."

Kristen couldn't wait to get home and share her news.

Chapter 32

That evening, Kristen and her parents met again as they had planned. She shared with them about how her coffee shop had been selected for the MBA project. She showed them the contract she had signed a few hours earlier. Dale was impressed with the detail that Kristen had already given to her plan and the initiative she had demonstrated in working with the MBA team.

He looked up at his daughter. "I just can't get over the change you have made. You used to be, and I say it in the most affectionate way, my 'no time for school' scatterbrained daughter."

Kristen grinned back. "I know. It almost seems like I have become like Jodie with her organizational lists." As soon as she said it, she wished she had not. Here she was again, comparing herself to her so very capable sister.

"Well, it looks like you have been doing your part," he said. "Now, let me tell you what I have been doing on my part."

Answering the doorbell, Bonnie ushered in an older man. "Kristen," Bonnie said, "we'd like you to meet Carl Harmon. Carl is the architect that your dad contacted."

Kristen quickly rose and went to meet the visitor. "Very pleased to meet you, Mr. Harmon. My dad spoke very highly of you." She extended her hand to the architect.

Carl smiled as he shook her hand. "Well, thank you. He spoke highly of you as well. You can call me Carl."

Dale invited him to join them at the table, and Carl spread out his drawings. "I found your proposed ideas very intriguing, and it was exciting to exercise my architectural muscles again. I hadn't realized that I had been missing some of that since I retired last year. Let me show you what I have designed based on what your father told me of your vision."

Over the next hour, Carl showed them drawing after drawing of the cafe, kitchen, bathrooms, and the potential eight apartments. He also had some ideas that would maximize the space in the apartments, allowing for a combination of studio and one-bedroom apartments. He even had a plan that would have fewer units, but all of them were two-bedroom apartments.

Taking in all the work that Carl had done, Kristen's head was swimming. Could this really become a reality? Did she have the skill to take on such an endeavor?

She was pulled back to the current conversation when she heard her father say, "I have talked to a few of the church leaders and asked them to begin praying about and discussing this idea. They have agreed to call a meeting with you next Tuesday."

Kristen realized the "you" to whom her father referred was herself. "Oh-uh, sure," she stammered. "Would it be too early to bring Carl along?"

Dale looked at Carl. "How about it? Would you be available?"

Carl grinned at them both. "I can be there!"

Saying her goodnights, Kristen retreated to her room to study.

Chapter 33

As the work on the Box Reno continued, Jodie could scarcely resist taking a peek. One morning, Jason saw her gazing at the basement door. "Oh, no, you don't, Miss Snoopy-Pants." He laughed.

"I know—it's just so tempting," she replied.

"Be strong! Resist temptation!" her husband lovingly commanded her. "I know what will take your mind off the Box Reno. Let's get that nursery started."

"But you can't get up the steps yet," Jodie argued.

"True, but we can plan it out. You know, decide paint colors, look at furniture—things like that."

"I would like to know whether the room will be for a boy or a girl before we paint it." Jodie ran her hand across her abdomen.

"When do we find out?"

"My doctor says she will schedule an ultrasound at any time after twenty weeks," Jodie replied.

"Are we there yet?" Jason questioned.

Jodie nodded. "Matter of fact, we are. Let's get it scheduled. I'll call today."

The crew arrived and headed to the basement. Soon, sounds of the air compressor and nail gun invaded the couple's conversation.

"Let's head to the family room and continue." Jason motioned to his wife.

As they passed the basement door, Jason stopped. "Do you realize that in another week and a half, I might be on crutches and can go down to the basement? That also means that I will be able to go upstairs and back to our bedroom."

"Yes!" Jodie beamed. "I don't think that had actually crossed my mind with all that has been going on. I'm going to love that!"

"And we can get rid of this bed in our family room, and we will have a normal house again." Jason waved his hand over the room before them.

"Well, let's get the plan into motion," replied Jodie as she grabbed the laptop. "Let me bring up a spreadsheet."

"Not saying a thing," Jason remarked as he smiled at her and shook his head. "Thank you for your organizational skills."

The next hour was spent outlining how to get rid of the bed and other hospital equipment that had occupied their house and making plans for their new nursery upstairs. They would need to move out the existing furniture from the guest room, choose a paint color, paint, get baby furniture, and then get it all set up as a nursery.

Jodie thought about the baby crib that was in her parents' attic. She had always assumed that, should Jason and she be blessed with a baby, their little one would sleep in that crib. Now that Kristen was also expecting, she wasn't so sure. Maybe her sister should have it. After all, she was older, and she was living at their parents' house. Yes, the crib should go to Kristen. It just seemed like the right thing to do. She would tell Kristen the next time she visited.

"Oh, wait," Jodie exclaimed. "Remember, Kristen got a crib for Christmas. She will most likely want to use the new one."

They decided they would give Kristen the choice. Jodie couldn't help but marvel about the change in her sister since Christmas Eve. Compared to the Kristen of last summer, one would never recognize her as even being the same person. It didn't seem possible, but even her looks had changed. Instead of a hard, steel look to her eyes and her tight-set jaw, there was now sparkle in her eyes and a softening to her features. Jodie took a moment to once again thank God for His transforming work in Kristen's life.

It seemed like Tuesday could not come fast enough, but finally, Jason and Jodie eagerly waited to see pictures of Baby Igland on the ultrasound screen. Her obstetrician opened the door and smiled at the couple. "Let's take a look at your little one, shall we?"

As the technician moved the probe across Jodie's abdomen, the doctor

Sisters of Crescent Valley

gave commentary on what was being displayed on the screen. Jason and his wife were amazed by the clarity of their baby's features and body.

"Okay, now the million-dollar question. I want to ask you both again, do you want to know the gender of your baby?" The doctor kept her eyes on the screen.

Jodie nodded and answered, "Yes, we both want to know."

"When we are determining the baby's gender from ultrasound, we not only look for the presence or absence of boy parts, but we also look for the presence of girl parts. She moved the pointer on the screen across the image. "Right here, your baby is a girl."

Both Jodie and Jason responded at the same time—Jodie with a squeal and Jason with "A girl! We are having a Jodie Junior!"

Jodie squeezed her husband's hand. "Are we going to tell the family?" Jason nodded.

"How do you think we should do it? Maybe another cake—one with pink inside?" Jodie asked.

The doctor interrupted their conversation with "I'm going to leave you to work out those details. Congratulations on your little baby girl. I will see you at your next appointment." With that, she left the room, while the technician cleaned Jodie's belly and gave instructions for their leaving.

On the way home, Jason and Jodie decided to have their gender reveal on the same day as the reveal of the Box Reno. They would get a little rocking chair to be placed in the kid area of the basement and put a pink baby blanket and a pink bear in the chair. Of course, neither Jodie nor Jason would be able to see it in place until the reveal, but they could get the chair ready upstairs, place it in a big black trash bag, and let the crew take it down, without opening the bag.

If Jason's surgery went well, he should be on crutches just before the reveals at a big party on February 2. They would ask Kristen if she would help by making some "groundhog" soup (her Tuscan sausage soup) and some biscuits. As they had previously decided, their guests would include their parents and Kristen, plus the renovation crew and their families. Jodie entered all the details on her new spreadsheet. They would make a call to Jason's parents later.

Jason's surgery went very smoothly as the surgeon removed the remaining external hardware. The physical therapist introduced a new group of at-home exercises that Jason needed to perform several times a day. His eagerness to get back to walking and, eventually, back to real work inspired Jason to pay close attention to all the instructions. He realized that he would be assuming much more personal responsibility for his recovery. His physical therapy appointments would be decreased to just once a week now, with his first visit in two days. At that visit, he would make the transition to crutches.

Jodie found the perfect little pink rocking chair, soft pink blanket, and the cutest pink bear dressed in ruffles and lace. She set it all up and placed it inside the large black trash bag. Tying the top shut, she placed it next to the basement door. The crew would be instructed that no one was allowed to look inside but to place the tied bag in the new kid area.

Chapter 34

K risten met with her MBA student team, and together they laid out a business plan for her. They made notes of the obstacles to her success, including the most obvious of financing the operation, getting approval from the church, the required permitting, her own pregnancy, and her classes. They agreed that Kristen would be responsible for the church approval and her personal issues, and they would work on the permitting and financial items. Her team would be investigating the restaurant laws as they applied to coffee shops and small cafes and searching out possible sources for financing. They had already investigated some business start-up groups that might be able and willing to assist with her beginning cash needs and loans. They observed, however, that her lack of any real assets would be a hindrance to her obtaining the money needed to begin. Kristen's assignment would be to evaluate the known obstacles and write her plans to address each. She knew she would be working diligently to get as much together as she could before the Tuesday meeting with the church leadership.

As she parked her car in front of Valley Edge Center of Hope on Tuesday evening, Kristen felt her confidence waning. She had all her notes and the architect's blueprints. She had tried to think of all the questions that might be asked of her and tried to formulate answers that would show the feasibility of her project. She sat there now, hands still on the steering wheel, and closed her eyes. The thought came into her head from out of nowhere. It seemed as if she could almost hear someone saying, "Wait a minute there, Kristen. I don't think this is your project. It belongs to Me. Have you forgotten that you gave Me the steering wheel of your life?"

Kristen opened her eyes and looked at her hands gripping the car's steering wheel. She deliberately let go of the wheel and opened her palms to the sky. She spoke her confession aloud. "God, just like I was grasping the steering wheel of this car, I was grasping the steering wheel of this coffee shop and project. I am now handing this over to You. Help me to always remember that. Whether the leaders agree to the project or turn it down, I trust that You will direct my life the way You want. I have always tried to control everything, but I give that control to You. Help me tonight to explain the project in the way that You would want."

By the time Kristen picked up her packet of materials, she experienced a new peace that could have only come from God. She smiled and whispered, "Thank You," as she entered the church and made her way to the group that was gathered at a large table in the lobby.

She smiled at her father and noticed Carl was there, just as he had promised. She recognized Pastor Ron, of course, but did not know any of the rest of the leaders seated at the table. All the men at the table stood as she came to the table, and Pastor Ron motioned toward one of the empty chairs. "Welcome, Kristen. Why don't you have a seat here? We are about ready to begin. We are just waiting on Joyce Martin and Ted Jarrelson. They should be here any minute."

No sooner had Pastor Ron said the words than the door opened, and both missing leaders entered. Kristen observed that, again, the men rose when Joyce approached the table. That, she thought, was not something that was done very often anymore in our society. In fact, she was quite sure that she had never experienced that before. She wasn't sure if the practice was a good thing or a bad thing, but it did feel pretty good. It made her feel honored. The group all introduced themselves and said what they did as a part of the church, or fellowship, as they called it.

Pastor Ron asked Dale to give a summary of the purpose of the meeting and then hand it over to his daughter. Kristen reminded herself of the steering wheel as she took a deep breath and began to explain the vision she had for the coffee shop / cafe and the related apartments and program. She deferred to Carl to explain the blueprints. He did an excellent job emphasizing the practical aspects of his plans. As all was being explained, Kristen carefully watched the faces of the leadership team. She thought she detected a certain openness to the idea, but she could also sense some reservations. The project was then opened to discussion and questions. The questions included financing, labor, timelines, oversight, the role of the MBA student team, and goals. At the end of the discussion, Pastor Ron stated that there would be no decisions made tonight but that everyone was to spend the next week praying about it.

Ted said, "Let's spend some time right now praying that God will direct our thoughts, ideas, and decisions concerning this." Then, one by one, each of the leaders prayed for God's will. Kristen was somewhat surprised at the way each of the leaders expressed their willingness to do what God wanted in this matter. All at once, Kristen realized that they were praying, in order, around the table, and there was only one person between her and the person who was currently praying. Would she be expected to pray? Apparently so. Her thoughts shifted from the words the person was now praying to what in the world she would say when her turn came. She had never prayed in front of a group before. Her stomach began to churn as she grew more distressed. Once again, the steering wheel picture came to her mind. Here she was, trying to grab at the wheel—even in the act of talking to God. She looked at her hands, now clenched in her lap, and she opened them again, palms up. She silently prayed, "God, You've got this!"

When her turn came, she prayed simply and sincerely, "God, You know that I have struggled with the control of my life. I thank You for Your continued reminders to me to let go of the steering wheel and let You take full control. I give this coffee shop, the apartments, and the whole project to You. I give You the decisions, the timetables, and the funding. Help me to be the follower and to honor You. I pray this in the name of Jesus. Amen."

Before they adjourned, all agreed to meet again in one week.

Pastor Ron turned to Carl. "I want to thank you for all of the work you have done on the plans and blueprints and your willingness to meet with us tonight. I want to extend an invitation to you to come to all the meetings until this project is completed."

Carl thanked the pastor and the leadership team. He said he would be honored to be a part of this exciting, new venture.

The pastor then turned to Kristen. "And you, young lady, have brought to us a great vision for the expansion of our ministry to this community.

Thank you for bringing this project to us for consideration. You are not only welcomed to all the meetings, but you will be an essential part of each meeting. Can you make such a commitment?"

"What else do I have to do?" Kristen smiled. "You don't know what this means to me. I never dreamed that my life would be so much different than it was last fall or that I would be involved in anything this phenomenal. Thank you, everyone!"

Chapter 35

The day finally came for the Box Reno reveal and the big party. The couple decided that they would get to see the basement by themselves first for a few minutes before the whole gang came down. They would uncover the chair then.

Kristen agreed to make her version of Tuscan sausage soup in honor of Groundhog's Day. She said she would also bring a pot of her chicken vegetable and noodle soup, just in case someone did not care for sausage. She volunteered to bake her flaky layered rolls. Jodie ordered a cherry cake decorated with a pink baby carriage.

With all the plans in place, Jason and Jodie headed off to the appointment that would give him back his freedom to navigate steps. All went well as Jason was fitted with a new brace and issued a pair of crutches. The physical therapist made sure that Jason was steady on his crutches, and he was given special instructions about snow and ice. He was taught how to navigate stairs by using the handrail, along with a crutch. He was told that his next step up, in about a month, would be a cane. He found out that he would also be starting some hydrotherapy so that the pool water could help to support his weight as he exercised the muscles that had been so restricted. The best news was that his doctor thought Jason's surgery in March would be his last.

Excitement grew as they headed home. Jodie couldn't figure out which part of their evening celebration was the most exciting—Jason's being able to walk with crutches, her seeing the Box Reno for the first time, or the revealing that their baby was a girl. The whole event would be magnificent.

They picked up the cake from the bakery and decided that they would hide it in the mudroom until the big reveal.

Kristen was the first to arrive, making several trips to her car to bring in her contributions to the evening—three big pots of soup and a large basket of rolls. The rest of the guests arrived in short order, with each joining in the exciting conversations.

"There is one thing, I guess, that we had not decided," Jason stated, looking at his wife. "When are we doing the Box Reno reveal? Now or after we have soup?"

"Oh, let's do it now!" Jodie squealed. "I can't bear to wait any longer!"

"Okay, now it is. Here's the deal—since neither Jodie nor I have seen the basement yet, and it will take me a while to navigate the steps, I would like for just the two of us to go down first. Give us a few minutes to enjoy it, and then we will call the rest of you down."

Everyone agreed, and the couple made their way to the door.

"This is it!" Jodie practically danced as they descended the stairs. Jason did a great job, following his instructions to use the handrail and one crutch to support his weight.

They took in the transformation of The Box, remarking on many of the details. Jodie spotted the kid area and the big black plastic-covered chair. She quickly removed the bag and placed the chair so it would be readily noticed. Stuffing the bag into a trash can, she called up the stairs, "You can all come down! You won't believe what these guys have done!"

The troop made their way down, led by Jodie's parents, then her sister, and then the guys from the crew and those who came with them.

They all admired the fireplace and the family area.

"How did you get a pool table in here without my knowing it and how did you fit that into our budget?" Jason eyed Matt.

Matt grinned as big of a smile as anyone had ever seen. "Well, it isn't brand-new. I had a friend who was upgrading his table, and when I told him of this project, he let me have it for nothing."

"Amazing, man!" Jason replied as he slapped his buddy on the back. "Rest assured that I'll be hosting many a game here."

"We're counting on that!" Phil interjected.

Just then, Jodie's mother turned toward the cute kid area. "Oh! Oh! Oh!" she gasped. "Look! Look, Dale! There's a little pink rocking chair, a pink blanket, and a ruffly pink bear! I think we are having a granddaughter!"

They rushed to hug Jason and Jodie.

Kristen looked at the chair, and immediately, some of the old thoughts came flooding in. *A granddaughter—is that better than a grandson?* If Jodie had a son, would that put her own baby in direct competition? Maybe it would be better if they were different. She wasn't sure why she always felt like she was competing with Jodie. Now, would their babies pick up that same competition? Even with all the changes that had taken place within her, she didn't know if she could ever get past this. She pulled herself together and went to the little rocking chair. Picking up the pink bear, she forced a smile at her sister. "Congratulations, again! Now the parents will have a matched pair—a grandson and a granddaughter." As soon as she said it, she realized that she had not told any of the rest of the crew about her pregnancy. She quickly drew in a breath, but she supposed that, by now, Matt or Jason had probably told them. And her growing baby bump could hardly hide the fact anyway.

Jodie smiled back at her. "Yeah, I just know the cousins will be great friends!"

The soups were delicious, and the conversation was animated. Talk moved from the Box Reno to baby talk, to Jodie's hospital work, to the Tackner stable landscaping project, and to Kristin's coffee shop vision. Matt told of how his mother wanted him to renovate her kitchen and bring it into the twenty-first century. Kristen couldn't keep herself from sneaking glances at him as they all sat at the tables. When the cake was brought in, everyone again celebrated the expectation of the birth of a baby girl.

Chapter 36

B y the time the Valley Edge Center of Hope's leadership team met again to discuss the proposal for the coffee shop / apartment project, several members had been working on various tasks to move things along. Joyce had made contacts with several agencies that worked with individuals and families that were trying to make new starts in their lives. She discovered that, while there was some government assistance to be had, such assistance came with quite a few restrictions. She had concluded that, if possible, Valley Edge should try to avoid that kind of financial entanglement. Carl had contacted some of his friends in construction and in building supply and had obtained tentative commitments of substantial amounts of donated resources and labor. As he told the team of these conversations, he spoke of the interest and excitement these professionals expressed for the project. He related that each of them had a story to tell of someone in his or her own life who could have benefitted from a program like the one that was being proposed. Others identified electricians, plumbers, and others who could be asked to help.

Jon Clarington, the church's treasurer, had investigated the legal ramifications of expanding their ministry into the area of providing housing, being a landlord, and running the coffee shop as a nonprofit business. He related that their lawyer confirmed that by forming a separate nonprofit agency under the umbrella of the church, and if they followed the nonprofit laws, they could do all of this without jeopardizing their existing nonprofit status.

As others spoke, it was soon evident that all were on board with proceeding with the project. They established a project committee consisting of Kristen, Joyce, Carl, and Jon. This committee would be meeting weekly to keep the project moving ahead. It was decided that, even though he did not attend Valley Center, Carl would be a terrific addition to the committee because of his passion for the project and because they wanted the project to be embraced by the larger community. Joyce was appointed as chairperson of the committee and was instructed to email a weekly summary of activity to the members of the leadership team. Kristen and Carl would also attend the regularly scheduled monthly church leadership meetings, where the committee would give a report and answer any questions.

As they closed the meeting in prayer, Kristen could hardly contain her gratitude for all that had happened. The speed at which the project was moving forward was, in itself, a miracle.

Over the next few weeks, the diligent committee finalized the remodel plans for the coffee shop / cafe. It would include both a drive-up window and an adjoining combination classroom / break room / study room. This room could be used for training the employees and for outreach classes to the community, as well as a place for the college students to study and a place for babies of employees who were young mothers. They decided that the coffee shop would be named Grounds for Hope. The apartments would be named Living Hope, and the training provided for the residents would be called the New Hope Project. Each week, Kristen brought the suggestions from the MBA student group, and the committee intently examined all the recommendations. By the time of the next leadership team meeting, the committee could not contain their excitement to present all that had been accomplished.

The leadership team approved the name choices and made available some initial funding for the build-out of the coffee shop and its associated kitchen area, restrooms, and classroom. Much of the construction work would be done in the evenings, as many of the contractors, plumbers, electricians, and carpenters were donating time after their regular workdays. Carl volunteered to act as the general contractor for the project, and he agreed to be on site as often as possible whenever others were there to work. Joyce and Kristen were to work together to obtain the needed tables, chairs, kitchen supplies, and paper goods.

Kristen soon discovered that what she was learning in her dry accounting class was just what she needed. Keeping track of the budget, expenses, volunteer labor, and timelines was almost more than she could do. She found herself scheduling some out-of-class time with her accounting professor. Nobody was more shocked by this than Kristen. She was amazed that the class that she thought was the most boring was the one that she needed the most. While the entrepreneur class was inspiring and put her in contact with her MBA group, the class was totally focused on the money-making potential of a business and how to get rich. Somehow, "profit" and "nonprofit" did not operate in the same world. Other conflicting ideas were "millionaire" versus "ministry" and "power" versus "people."

Paul Winters had seemed interested in Kristen, but he soon discovered that her lack of vision for a real money-making business was not very appealing to him. After a few weeks, he had set his sights on a student who was designing her own line of boutique sportswear. She, he discovered, had already made over $500,000 in her first six months of online sales.

With her studies, the weekly committee meeting, the meetings with her MBA group, the monthly leadership team meetings, and all the legwork she had to do for the project, Kristen soon found herself running out of steam. Her mother suggested that she try to slow down a bit, as the combination of lack of sleep and added stress was not good for the baby. While Kristen agreed with her, she struggled to make any changes in her hectic routine. She continued to burn the midnight oil, trying to decide how to make the tightly scheduled timeline work.

Chapter 37

Matt and Jason worked together to bring the new remodeling branch of Igland's into reality. The early-spring sunshine streamed in through the window as they pored over spreadsheets and design books. Their intensity was interrupted by the doorbell.

As Jason rose to answer the door, he turned back to Matt. "Business always seemed so easy, but suddenly it has become a lot more complicated. I think one of us should have joined Kristen in some of her classes."

Jason opened the door. "And look who it is!" he exclaimed. "Come on in, Kristen. We were just saying that some of the classes you are taking might be of help to us."

Matt looked up and smiled at Kristen. She held a box of what could only be some delectable treats to accompany their coffee. He couldn't help but notice that her protruding belly had seemed to have grown appreciably since he had last seen her.

"I created a couple of new recipes. I have some dark chocolate cranberry muffins and some almond scones. I need to see if they pass the test from my favorite tasters." Kristen set the box on the table and lifted the lid. The mixtures of the aromas prompted the men to breathe deeply.

"You never disappoint me, Kristen." Matt grinned as he reached for an almond scone.

Kristen blushed and stammered, "I hope you like them." Matt's words echoed in her brain. *You never disappoint me.* She realized he was speaking only of the baked delights. Of course, she disappointed him in other areas; she had disappointed everyone with the choices that she had made in life. She had disappointed her parents. She had disappointed Jodie and

Jason. She had disappointed Pete. She had disappointed herself. She had disappointed God. The old guilt began to rise in her heart. Quickly she turned and fled to the kitchen. Once there, she collapsed into a chair at the island. She knew that the men in the next room would hear her if she started to cry, but she couldn't contain the tears that trickled from her eyes. Would she ever be able to rid herself of the feelings of guilt that continued to plague her?

Matt looked up from the project. "What if I did take some classes?"

"How would you be able to make classes fit into your schedule?" Jason questioned.

"I'm thinking that I could maybe find some online courses that I could work on at my own pace."

"What would you take?"

Matt looked thoughtful as he took a more than polite bite of a chocolate cranberry muffin. "I am thinking we need to work on small business expansion and maybe some business accounting. I was never an overachiever in school, but I think I might have a bit more motivation now." Matt glanced toward the kitchen. "Maybe Kristen would know where I could pick up some online courses."

"Hey, Kristen!" Jason called. "Could you come out here a moment?"

Kristen quickly composed herself. "Sure, uh—just give me a second or two. I am getting a cup of coffee."

The looks on the men's faces gave Kristen a moment of hesitation. Cheesy grins gave them the appearance of two schoolboys who had just hatched up a scheme to pull a prank at recess time.

"What in the world is up with you guys?" Kristen said.

"Well, first of all," Jason replied, "these muffins and scones are over the top."

"They sure are. I have already had one of each." Matt smiled. "The second thing is that I am thinking of taking some business courses to help us out as we expand the business into remodeling. I was hoping you might be able to recommend some courses."

Kristen hesitated. "Me? I just got started, but the courses that I am taking at the junior college are pretty good."

"Do you know if they offer any online courses?"

"I think they do. I am not sure which ones or when they are offered.

The entrepreneur class I am taking is geared toward starting your own business, but the accounting class has been surprisingly helpful to me." Kristen tilted her head as she looked at her brother-in-law's business partner.

In response, Matt tilted his own head to match hers.

Narrowing her eyes and pursing her lips, she said to Matt, "Are you mocking me?"

Matt gave a short laugh and replied, "Not at all. It was cute." He laughed again. "Maybe I'll head over to the college this afternoon and find out what it would take for me to get into a flexible online accounting class."

"I am going there this afternoon myself. Maybe I could show you around."

Nodding, Matt smiled. "That would be great. Are you free around one thirty?"

"Works for me!" Kristen turned again to the kitchen. "Want to meet me there?"

"Sure! It's a date!" Matt caught himself. "I mean, yes, we can meet then."

As Kristen returned to the kitchen, she tried to dismiss the new thoughts that came rushing into her head. Even though it did not carry the intent, "It's a date" coming from Matt—fine, upstanding, Christian, hardworking, moral, thoughtful, motivated, kind Matt—stuck in her brain. The adjectives just seemed to cascade in, and her brain was flooded with images that never could be. Why, oh why, had she messed up her life so badly? If only she had not turned away from God. If only she had not allowed herself to become intimate with so many men. If only she was not now expecting a child. If only—then maybe she might have had a chance with Matt. Her flood of thoughts was beginning to drown her. If only things were different.

Kristen went back to her parents' house and did some studying on her accounting. At one o'clock, she gathered her books into her backpack and left for the college to meet Matt. She had come to grips that she and Matt may, indeed, have a chance to be friends, but there could never be anything more. The position of Matt's special someone would be reserved for a young lady of character and one who had kept herself pure. After all, that was what he deserved.

At the college, Kristen directed Matt to the academic counseling offices. She took care of her tuition payment and then found a seat back by the offices. She remembered sitting there just a few months ago, waiting for her appointment with the counselor. She had been scared, confused, and so unsure of her future. Now, it looked like there could be a future for her. Plans were falling into place for the Grounds for Hope coffee shop and for the Living Hope apartments. She couldn't help but smile when she thought about how far she had come. As soon as her own apartment was ready, she would be moving out of her parents' place. And, sure, there was still a baby boy who would soon be entering the world and giving her more responsibility than she had ever imagined. She felt so mature and so immature all at the same time.

Chapter 38

J odie had not felt well all day at work. She hoped that she was not coming down with something. But as Jason had said many times, "What do you expect when you work with sickies every day?" She was glad to say goodnight to everyone and leave for home. The pain in her back continued to plague her on her drive home. She placed the back of her hand against her forehead and then her cheek. No, she didn't have a fever. She chuckled a bit as she thought about the fact that she was a medical professional, and her method for checking for fever was the back of her hand. She imagined how that would look in a patient's chart. "Temperature: felt like about 102.6 degrees." But, she reasoned, it had, indeed, worked for hundreds of years. Oh, the pain returned. Perhaps a nice warm bath would help her muscles to relax.

Jodie soon realized that the pains she was having were not related to any disease state—she was having Braxton-Hicks contractions, those contractions that commonly happen in the last few months of pregnancy. She still had a couple of months to go, but she had been on her feet all day, and that was probably what had brought them on. She would just go home, put her feet up, and relax with a nice cup of chamomile tea. The leftover meatloaf from last night would make some great sandwiches. Jason had always enjoyed those. And she would open a can of green beans. That would be easy and satisfying.

When Jodie turned into the drive, she was surprised and pleased to see Jason's truck. He must have completed his most recent small job in Crescent Heights. While they had not yet completed the Tackner stable landscaping, they had been able to dovetail in some of these smaller projects. The way his reputation had spread in that development was nothing short of amazing. As neighbor talked to neighbor, more were engaging Igland Landscaping to contract its services. Some of the jobs were small and could be completed in a few days by one or two workers, while others demanded weeks of an all-hands-on-deck crew. The major projects were scheduled to follow the Tackner job.

Jodie gathered her lunch bag and purse and entered the house. "I'm home!"

Jason answered from the kitchen, "I'm in here. I was just checking to see if there was anything that I could fix for dinner."

"I was just thinking about the same thing, and I thought we could have meatloaf sandwiches." Jodie gasped and grabbed her back.

Jason rushed to her side and hugged her. "What is it? Are you okay?"

Struggling for a breath, Jodie responded, "Yes. I'm okay. I'm just having some Braxton-Hicks contractions."

"You told me about those. Those are the false labor ones. Right?"

"Yeah, it's not time for the real thing." Jodie laughed a bit and continued, "We don't have to run to the hospital yet."

"So do you need to lie down?"

"No, but I think I will sit here a while and get my feet up. I overdid a bit today at the hospital. We had a rather wild day."

Jason escorted his wife to the recliner and helped her into it. "Can I bring you something to drink?"

"That would be nice. On the way home, I was thinking that a cup of hot chamomile tea would taste really good. That might help me to relax."

"On my way to prepare your tea, Madame." He made a sweeping bow in Jodie's direction.

Jodie grinned at her husband and chortled. "Come back here! And please don't call me Madame. That makes me feel incredibly old."

Jason bent over and kissed Jodi's forehead. "Then I will say, 'On my way to prepare your tea, my dear!'" To Jodie's delight, he made another bow on his way back to the kitchen.

While Jason brewed her tea, Jodie lay back and closed her eyes. The softness of the chair felt so good, and having her feet up was just what she needed. Once she had her tea, her whole body could relax. Her back was already feeling better.

Jason returned with the steaming cup. He picked up a coaster from the shelf and placed it on the end table next to the chair.

"Would you like the remote so you can watch the news or something?"

"No, I think I will just enjoy the peace and quiet."

"You do that then. I will go carve up the meatloaf into slices. Do you want yours with mayo and mustard?"

"Yes, please. And how about a dill pickle spear?"

"I thought you were supposed to be past those cravings," Jason teased.

Jodie returned a playful smirk. "This isn't a craving. I have always liked dill pickles. You know that."

"I was just trying to get that smile from you."

"Did you get it?" Jodie smiled.

"I did—twice."

"Would you like to heat up some green beans to go with the sandwich?"

"That sounds good. I was just thinking I might open a bag of Cheetos as well."

"Umm! Perfect cuisine," Jodie replied. She rested her head back on the chair as Jason left to prepare the meal.

She hadn't realized how very tired she was, but soon Jodie was slumbering peacefully in the chair. Another pain woke her. This one was stronger and lasted longer.

"Jason," she called.

Jason answered from the kitchen, "Is something wrong?"

"I'm not sure. I know our little girl is not due for another seven weeks, but ..."

Concern clouded Jason's face as he came to Jodie's side. He grabbed her hand. "Do you think this is more than the Brax-thing?"

"Maybe. Something just doesn't feel right."

"Well, let's go get you checked out. We don't want to stay here and let something go wrong."

Jodie gave a weak smile and squeezed his hand.

"You wait here. Tell me what I should get together for you." Jason looked deep into his wife's eyes. "Everything is going to be okay."

"I know." Jodie nodded. "God is in control, and He loves us."

"Now, what do I need to get?"

"Umm, let me think. Can you pack one change of clothes for yourself and a robe and underwear for me? And toiletries for each of us. If our little one should decide to come now, we don't want her to wrinkle her cute little nose at her parents' bad breath."

"I'll get everything. You just stay there." Jason dashed up the stairs, not nearly as fast as he used to be able to do it, but still amazing himself at how well his body had healed and how quickly a man with a cane could move. He grabbed a small suitcase and hurriedly packed. In less than ten minutes, he was back down the stairs.

"Wow, that was fast!" Jodie exclaimed.

"Well, when I'm thinking of my wife and my little baby girl, I can't move fast enough. Ready?"

"Just a minute. Is there food sitting out in the kitchen?"

"Yeah, I need to put that away," Jason answered as he headed that way.

"We certainly don't want Kristen thinking that I always leave food out when I go to the hospital. And, Jason, you might take your sandwich along. I know you are probably hungry."

"What about yours?"

"No, I don't think I should. Just wrap it and put it in the refrigerator."

Jason snatched up one of the sandwiches and the bag of Cheetos. He looked at the bag and decided to leave it behind because he didn't want to deal with orange fingers at the hospital. He glanced around to make sure everything was relatively cleaned up in the kitchen. The whole packing and cleaning process had been accomplished in short order.

"Ready?" he asked.

"As ready as I'll ever be." Jodie took a deep breath and got out of the chair.

"Do we need to call your OB doc?"

"Maybe I should. I do that on the way."

Jason, with a hand on his wife's back, carried the suitcase and a small lunch bag that held his meatloaf sandwich. Food was not what was on his mind as he set the bags in the back seat and got Jodie settled in. As he opened the door to get into the driver's seat, his silent prayer went up to his Father. "Dear God," he prayed, "we know that it is not time yet for our baby to be born. It is too early, and she is too little. We know that You are in control. Please, God, help us to trust You." Jason put the key into the ignition and headed back toward a place that had been all too familiar to his family in the past year.

Chapter 39

After undergoing an examination at the hospital, Jodie learned that her baby seemed determined to make an early entrance into the world. Jason held her tight as the doctor told them what they could expect. She explained about the team of people who would be assisting, the actual birth, the rush of activity, the incubator, and the whisking away of their baby as the premature infant team assessed and cared for her.

This was not the way Jodie had imagined the birth. She had assisted in several deliveries and had pictured her labor and the joyous birth. She would hold her little one on her chest and smother her with sweet kisses. She had imagined that Jason would be there and would be kissing Jodi's forehead while he was stroking his daughter's head and back. That was the way it was supposed to be.

All those images now were replaced with a flurry of activity as nurses and assistants hurried to get everything in place. The electronic fetal monitor showed a strong and steady heartbeat. Jodie watched the top heartbeat line and the lower contraction line. The baby was tolerating the labor well.

"Fight, little one," Jodie said. "You're going to make it." Jodie willed all her strength to her baby.

Jason reached for his wife's hand. "I know this isn't how we had planned it, but it's all going to be okay. This is no surprise to God."

Jodie nodded, tears filling her eyes.

Jason bent over and kissed Jodi's forehead. Jodie smiled and thought, *There is one part of the picture, at least.*

Dr. Jennifer Segu came back to reexamine her patient. "We probably have several hours to go, but things are progressing nicely. Let me know if the pain level becomes too great. I can get you something to help you be more comfortable."

"I'm doing okay so far," Jodie responded. "I'm just so concerned about our baby."

"I know you are," the doctor answered as she looked over the printout from the monitor. "She is going to be just fine. She will need a little help for a few weeks, but she will get there."

Jason turned to Jodi. "I think I will step out and call your parents to let them know that they are going to have a grandbaby sooner than they thought."

"That's a good idea," Dr. Segu said. "And if you haven't already eaten, you might get yourself something while you are at it. We don't need to have a starving dad passing out during the delivery."

"Are you okay with that?" Jason asked Jodi.

"Yes, I'm in good hands," Jodie responded. "Oh—here we go again." Her voice caught as she breathed in response to another contraction.

"Are you sure you don't want me to stay?"

"No, you go. Dr. Segu said it's going to be several hours yet. Just don't be gone too long."

Jason nodded and left for the cafeteria. As he poured a cup of coffee, he felt fortunate that he had not gotten to the age where caffeine kept him awake at night. He had a feeling that he wouldn't be sleeping tonight anyway. He ate his meatloaf sandwich and pondered the future. Silently, he prayed for their little girl, "Please, God, help our tiny baby. Help her lungs to breathe and everything else to work right. Protect her tiny brain from complications." Jason could not remember a time when he had prayed so desperately—not even after his accident. This, he realized, must be what it means to be a father, what it means to care for a child even more than one cares for his own life. He was jerked back to reality when a hand touched his shoulder.

Jason turned.

"Hi. Do you remember me?"

The smiling face did look familiar, but Jason's brain was otherwise occupied. "I think I do, or maybe, more correctly, I think I should. You came to visit when I was in Orthopedics."

"Yes. I'm Selma."

Jason returned her kind smile. "I remember now. Selma. It's good to see you."

"Are you visiting someone here?" Selma asked.

"Not exactly. Jodie is down in Labor and Delivery," Jason responded.

"Wow! Already? I didn't realize she was that close. I just saw her a few days ago."

Jason's face clouded. "Well, that's the problem. She is not due yet. We still have about eight weeks to go. Our baby girl is premature."

Concern spread in Selma's eyes. "I'm so sorry. But, you know, Jason, that thirty-two-week babies have really good chances. They will be prepared for her and will take excellent care of her."

"I know all of that. That's what Jodie told me." Jason nodded. "It's just really personal when it is your own baby. I'm sorry, but I need to get back to Jodie."

"I'll be praying for you. You can trust God." Selma again placed her hand on Jason's shoulder.

"Thanks. My head knows that He is in control. My heart just needs to catch up." Jason choked out the words as he rose. "I need to go."

With that, Jason tossed his cup into the huge trash can and headed back to the birthing center.

Labor continued to progress slowly. Their little girl, however eager to make her entry into the world, now seemed to be dragging her feet. The process was beginning to take its toll on Jodie. The contractions were consistent and getting stronger. There was scarcely enough time between contractions now for Jodie to recover from one before another began. After her last examination, Dr. Segu suggested an epidural, and Jodie agreed. It had already been eight hours since the couple had arrived at the hospital. Jason was glad he had had that cup of coffee. The labor had been stressful for both. He was glad that the epidural had the desired effect and that Jodie was now much more comfortable. Even though the contractions still were evident on the monitor, Jodie was no longer feeling the pain. She was able to catch a few cat naps while her body prepared for the birth.

Shortly before sunrise, the nurse announced, "Jodie, Jason, it's time!"

The couple, now wide awake, looked at each other in disbelief. Jason held his wife's hand and bent over to kiss her. "Sweetheart, let's meet our little one."

Jodie nodded as the nurse lowered the end of the bed and adjusted Jodie to a half-sitting position. The nurse glanced another time at the monitor. "Dr. Segu is scrubbing up, along with the special neonatal team. They will all be here in just a few minutes."

No sooner had she said that than the activity level in the hall increased. There was a jumble of voices and the sound of carts. One of the staff came in and introduced herself. "Hi, I'm Heather. I am what they call a scribe. I will be writing chart notes during your delivery. Since there will be so many people and pieces of equipment in here, I will be right outside the door. Do you have any questions about what I will be doing?"

"No," Jodie answered. "I am a nurse, so I am acquainted with your job."

"Excellent. I'll clear out then."

As Heather left to position herself outside, others entered the room. They all introduced themselves and assumed their places. There was an anesthesia cart, followed by scrubbed personnel, an incubator, and finally Dr. Segu. Jodie recognized the neonatal crash cart out in the hallway. This, she assumed, was the standard procedure for premature deliveries, but seeing it unnerved her. Her heart cried out again to God.

After a few moments and as many pushes, new life entered the world. Dr. Segu immediately handed the little form to Dr. Anderson, the neonatologist specializing in premature babies. Jodie longed to hold her new baby, but she knew she could not do that right now. Her baby needed the care of professionals. Her eyes, however, stayed fixed on the tiny wriggling body. Then she heard it—the sound a new mother longs to hear—the voice of her child. It wasn't a lusty wail, but it was more like a whimper or like the cry of a kitten, but it was her. Tears began to flow down Jodie's face, and she was hardly aware of anything else in the room. Jason slipped his arm under Jodie's head and hugged her tightly. "She is here. Our beautiful little girl is here!"

Dr. Anderson looked up at the couple. "We are going to take this precious little one to the neonatal ICU now, but I want you to get a good look at her before we go. You can each touch her hand for a second. Say hello to your baby girl."

After their ever too brief exchange, the neonatal team whisked away the incubator that cradled its fragile cargo.

Chapter 40

D ale and Bonnie made their way to the birthing center room that had been assigned to Jodie. As soon they opened the door, Jodie spotted them and smiled broadly. After hugs and kisses, Jason began to tell them of the events of the last fourteen hours.

"We called Kristen, as you asked," Bonnie stated. "She said she would stop by right after her classes.

"And I called Matt. He is taking charge of the guys today. He said he knew exactly what they needed to be doing," Dale added.

"He's the best right-hand man I could ever have," Jason said. "He has always come through for me."

Jodie nodded, her eyes getting heavy from the lack of sleep.

Bonnie noted the tiredness of her daughter. "Dale, I think we need to go for now. Jodie is really tired."

"It looks like Jason is also in need of some sleep. We will be back this afternoon." Dale bent to kiss Jodie.

"They said that we should get to go down and see our baby in a few hours. I don't know when the rest of the family will get to see her," Jodie informed her parents.

"We will wait—impatiently to be sure." Bonnie smiled. "But, you know, I think that darling little girl of yours needs a name. I'm getting rather tired of calling her Little Baby."

Jodie laughed. "I know. We're getting close to deciding. By the time you get back, I think she should have a name."

"That will make the wait even more impossible," Bonnie said with a chuckle.

Waking from their short naps, Jason and Jodie were greeted by a CNA with a wheelchair. "Are you ready to take a short trip down to the NICU? I understand you have someone there who is ready for your visit."

"Been waiting for this," Jason answered.

The sights and sounds of the neonatal ICU were foreign to Jason. Even though Jodie had been there during her internship, it was so different now that her own baby was a patient. The lights, for the most part, were dimmed and the sounds muted to decrease the external stimulation for those who could not wait until term. Their eyes darted around the room and noted that there were four babies in residence. They spotted an incubator in the middle of the room with the name "IGLAND" at the top. The CNA wheeled Jodie up to the side of the incubator. "Here you go. The nurse will be right with you."

Jason and Jodie immediately looked at their baby's little face. "She is so beautiful," Jason said.

"She is."

"Just like her mother," he continued as he reached down and kissed his wife.

"Excuse me," a voice said. "I don't want to intrude on a private moment, but I do want to introduce you to someone very special. I know you had a brief glimpse after delivery, but I have the privilege of making the formal introductions. Mr. and Mrs. Igland, this is Baby Girl Igland—until we have a more fitting name for her. Little one, meet your parents. I think you are going to like them."

Jodie finally lifted her eyes to see the nurse, identified as Bethany M. by her name tag. The nurse punched keys on the mobile computer on a stand. "This baby has been a welcomed addition to our little neonatal family. She will spend a few weeks here before she comes home to you. Let me explain what we are doing now and what you can expect during the time she is here."

Bethany explained all the different monitors and the lines attached to them. The instruments would track the baby's breathing, heartbeat, and temperature. The oxygen sensor would monitor how well her lungs were working to get oxygen out to the rest of her body. She pointed out the tubing that was attached to her scalp and ran up to a small IV bag. They would use this line to administer most of the medications the baby might need. Bethany told them of the possible complications that preemies faced. Jodie felt that all this information was a bit overwhelming, and she was an RN. She realized how difficult this must be for parents who had no medical background. Her attention went back to Bethany as she explained the expected timetable and the milestones that would indicate the progress their baby would be making.

After they returned to Jodie's room, Jason asked, "Well?"

"Well, what?" Jodie responded.

"Well, what name shall we choose now that we have gotten to really meet her? She is so incredibly beautiful!"

"Ever since they told us that she would be arriving early, I've been thinking about Hope—that was one of the names on our shortlist. I also know that it's being used for Grounds for Hope and Living Hope. Is it too much?" Jodie looked for her husband's reaction.

"I think Hope is perfect." He smiled. "I had been thinking the very same thing. And, anyway, you can never have too much hope."

"I'm so glad you agree. But if it's okay with you, I think Hope should be her middle name."

"So—not Hope?"

"We can call her Hope, but I would like her first name to be Elsa—after Mormor Lindstrom. It sounds right—Elsa Hope Igland. It flows better than Hope Elsa Igland."

Jason tilted his head a bit and ran the names through his mind. Looking back at Jodie, he nodded. "I like it. Elsa Hope Igland it is." He reached to take his wife's hand and smiled. "Let's share this news with God."

"I think He might already know." Jodie laughed.

The two of them, with their foreheads touching and their hands clasped in each other's, prayed together, thanking their heavenly Father again for the safe delivery of their dear Elsa Hope and asking for His care for her in the days and weeks to come.

Chapter 41

Kristen tried to keep her concentration on her assignments and all that needed to be done for the coffee shop. Making these tasks even more difficult was the ever-present reminder that she could give birth at any time, especially since Jodie had already delivered. As she considered this, her brain jumped back to that old familiar spot where she competed with her younger sister. Now Jodie had her baby. True, the baby was premature and in the NICU. True, Jodie would have to go home without her baby. True, her bonding time with her baby would be in a controlled environment with lots of people and activity surrounding her. True, she and Jason would not be able to enjoy evenings at home together with their baby for some time to come. But Jodie's baby had arrived first. She was here to receive the sole attention of her grandparents. She would always be the first grandbaby. Jodie had a home of her own, she had a husband of her own who also had his own business, she had a well-paying, meaningful job in which she was highly respected, and now she had her own baby. Oh, how Kristen wished that she could rid herself of these recurring comparative and competitive thoughts. Why did she struggle so much? She knew that these thoughts did nothing to help her, and she knew they were not what God desired for her. If she already knew this, why did they keep coming back to plague her?

She forced herself back to the capital expenditures sheets and reviewed the items on the list. As suggested by her MBA team, she had given the coffee shop and the apartments separate sheets. She knew that her final submission of the projected capital expenditures for the coffee shop was due next Tuesday. She closed her eyes to picture the shop in her mind.

Satisfied that she had accounted for all the furniture and equipment needed, she signed her name on the sheet and wrote the date. This was a practice that she had started to keep track of which sheets were still in process and which she had completed. Once she had signed it, she knew that sheet was completed. She placed the sheets back into her CapEx manila folder and filed it into her rolling crate. It seemed that the crate was her constant companion these days. She was making every effort to keep all her plans and accounting online, but for right now, paper seemed to be the best way for her to be able to address more than one sheet at a time. She just had to be careful to get her manual changes transferred to the online sheets.

Kristen knew that she had never been the excellent student her sister had been, so she was exceptionally pleased that her entrepreneurship class was going so well. Her work with her MBA team would soon be ending. A couple of her team members seemed to understand the "charity" and "nonprofit" nature of her business, but the others (her professor included) thought she was missing an opportunity to make some real money. She had been forced to think about the "ultimate" future of her "company" and where she envisioned it ten, twenty, and thirty years in the future. While others in the class expressed their plans to sell their company somewhere down the road and then either retire or begin another start-up, Kristen realized that approach would never be a part of her business model. She could, though, entertain the idea of helping other churches begin their own similar ministries. She was grateful that Paul had set his sights elsewhere and that he was no longer a distraction in class.

A glance at her calendar reminded her that she would need to find a time to meet with Joyce before the next project team meeting. While the MBA team provided her with the business acumen that she needed, the Valley Edge leadership team gave her the needed inspiration and encouragement to see the start-up succeed. She had never felt that she had to fight to defend her ideas, even when some asked for more details or further explanation. She sensed that the team members were truly there to assist and support her. That didn't mean that everything she suggested was put into action. Many times, changes were made to her plans, but they were made with careful reasoning. Joyce had been invaluable to her as they continued to meet on a weekly basis.

As she packed away her papers, she heard the familiar xylophone ring of her phone. Surprised, she noted that the call was coming from Meyers. The supervisor from when she had worked the night shift explained to her that she needed some temporary help for the next few weeks.

"So would this be of interest to you?" the supervisor asked.

"What exactly would the job entail? I am pretty far along in my pregnancy now."

"Oh, I didn't realize that you were pregnant." She paused a bit. "I think I could still use you to oversee logistics to make sure the work was progressing. It wouldn't involve any heavy lifting, although you would be on your feet for up to maybe a total of three to four hours."

"Hmm, let me think about it for a bit." Kristen said. "When would it begin, and what would be my hours?"

"We are planning to start this coming weekend—Friday night. It will be a night shift job. You would be working every Friday to Sunday night for three weeks. There may be another weekday night or two thrown in as we progress. We will be starting at 8:00 p.m. and working until 8:00 a.m.—a twelve-hour shift. I am hoping that would not be too long for you in your state right now." The anticipation of a positive response was evident in the supervisor's voice.

Without any further hint of commitment, Kristen said, "I know that Friday is coming soon, but when do you need to know?"

"As soon as possible, but I will definitely need an answer before noon tomorrow. I will need to go a temp agency if I don't hear from you by then."

"Okay. I will get back to you tomorrow morning. Let me sleep on it overnight. And I will pray about it."

"Pray about it? I didn't think you were the praying type." A laugh escaped the supervisor's mouth.

"Well, I wasn't when I was there with you, but a lot has changed for me since then. I can scarcely believe it myself." Kirsten smiled.

"Then I will leave you to your sleeping and praying, and I will expect a call tomorrow. Just call me back at this number. I'm hoping you will accept."

Once again, Kristen felt like there were too many thoughts swirling in her head. She knew she could use the money. She wanted to provide for herself and her baby. She didn't want to have to rely on others to supply the things she needed. She was feeling good, pregnancy-wise, and the hours would not interfere with her class or meeting schedules. She decided she would talk it over with her parents that evening. Right now, she needed to get herself over to the hospital to see her brand-new niece.

Chapter 42

Just before bed, Kristen plopped onto the couch in her parents' den. Dale and Bonnie were each in their favorite chairs, watching a reality show about teams trying to find a hidden treasure. At a commercial break, Kristen said, "I need some advice."

"This is truly a new MO for you, Kristen," her dad responded. "We have always loved you, but I must say I am really liking this new you."

"Well, I remind you that I am not the Kristen you knew, but I am the Kristen you know now."

Dale nodded. "You are indeed. Go on. What advice do you need? I just happen to have my virtual dad's bag of advice here with me."

"I've been offered a temporary, part-time job. It is just three weeks, Friday to Sunday nights at Meyers. It won't involve any heavy lifting, and I could really use the money. Being only weekends, it shouldn't interfere with my classes or meetings."

"So what are your concerns, honey?" Bonnie inquired.

"First is, even though it is not at the same time as my classes and meetings, I might have less time to work on my assignments and plans. But, then again, I could probably work more efficiently than I have been doing."

"It sounds like you have thought that one out and you could make it work. What else?" her mom asked.

"You know, I think I know where Jodie got at least some of her organizational skills. The next is whether or not I can do twelve-hour shifts with the baby and all."

"I think that is a legitimate concern," her mother said thoughtfully. "How have you been feeling?"

"Pretty well—except for that scare at Christmas. My doctor says that I am doing very well. I must say, though, that I am always ready for sleep when I hit the bed each night."

"It sounds like you are probably up for the challenge. You were able to handle those hours when you were early in your pregnancy, so I think you should be able to handle them now. I was able to work some pretty long shifts back when I was pregnant with you." Bonnie glanced toward her husband.

"And," her dad added, "if you find the hours are too long, maybe they would let you cut back a little."

"Yeah, I think that would work. I could do it."

"Anything else?" her mom questioned.

"I am hoping that I will feel up to going to church on Sundays after working a twelve-hour night shift." Kristen made a little face.

"That might be a struggle for you, but it is only for three Sundays," her dad said. "If you do get a little drowsy in church, I don't think anyone will hold it against you. I think you might have more problems on Mondays, trying to adjust to a daytime world again and going to classes."

"I hadn't thought of that." Kristen bit on her lower lip. "I just have to keep in mind that it is only three weeks. And like I said, I could really use the money."

"So have you decided to take the job?" Bonnie asked.

"Yes—wait a moment. Not yet."

"What else?" her parents asked at the same time.

"I told the supervisor that I wanted to sleep on it first, and I haven't done that yet. I also told her that I wanted to pray about it, and I haven't spent too much time doing that either." Kristen smiled as she got up from the couch. "Thanks so much, Mom and Dad, for helping me."

"That's what parents are here for." Her dad smiled back. "Or, at least, as I recently learned in a seminar, it is what parents of adult children are here for. We can listen, give advice when asked, pray for our children, and trust that they will make the right decisions."

"Sounds like that was a good seminar. I hope I will remember it when this little guy gets to be my age." Kristen rubbed her hand across her belly and then kissed each of her parents. "Good night!"

Kristen did spend some time talking with her heavenly Father about the job decision. She slept surprisingly well. Shortly after 9:00 a.m., she placed her call to accept the temporary position. She knew these next few weeks would be challenging, but she decided that it might be good training for the promised short nights she would have once her baby arrived.

Chapter 43

Over the next three weeks, Kristen's busy schedule began to take its toll. While she was pleased to have the extra money and the bit of overtime pay, she was relieved when the Meyers job ended. She tried to catch a few moments of sleep whenever she could.

Jodie's schedule was hectic in a totally separate way. Her days reminded her of Jason's hospitalization and how she was practically living at the hospital and going home only to shower and sleep. Along with that, there were now the hormonal changes and the pumping of milk for little Elsa Hope. Each morning, she would see Jason off to work and then drive to the hospital. She often caught a nap or two during her days at the hospital. Jason would join her there after work so they could spend some time together with Elsa Hope. They had decided that Jason should work a full schedule now and then take off time once their little girl came home.

Late one morning, Kristen met her sister at the hospital and took her out to a nearby deli cafe. Jodi told of the progress that Elsa Hope had been making. Thankfully, there had been no bleeding, and she was now breathing well on her own. The NICU milestones were slowly being checked off the list, and now she just needed to gain some more weight and be able to maintain her body temperature. She had been moved into the area of the NICU that was reserved for the more stable and progressing infants. There had been some talk of her being released in a few weeks—a bit ahead of the original predicted time.

"I love the name you chose for her—Elsa Hope. I think Mormor would have been pleased." Kristen took a bite of her smoked pork on rye sandwich.

"I like it too. We thought that we were going to call her Hope, but the longer we are with her, the more Jason and I are using both names, Elsa Hope." Jodie sipped her raspberry iced tea. "Her hair is starting to grow. I think it's going to be blonde, like yours."

"And like Mormor Lindstrom's was when she was a girl. I remember seeing pictures of her with her family." Kristen paused a moment. "Mom always said that I resembled her."

"I think you definitely do," Jodie replied. "You were such a beautiful little girl with your lovely blonde hair. Not to say that you aren't beautiful as an adult, because you still are."

"Thanks, sis!" Kristen took a deep breath and let the air out slowly. "I must say, though, I do not feel so very beautiful right now carrying this little guy around. I caught myself waddling a bit the other day. I had always told myself that I was never going to be one of those pregnant women who waddled."

They both laughed.

"You know that I am not glad that little Elsa Hope came early or that you are not getting to have her at home yet, but there are times that I feel a little envious that your baby is already here and has taken her place in our family." Kristen looked thoughtfully at her sister.

"I think I know what you are saying, Kristen. Listen, just because our babies came about in different ways and made or will make their entries into the world in different ways, they are equally special, and each will have an equally important place in our family." Jodie's voice conveyed the truth of her words.

"Thank you, sis." Kristen hugged Jodie. "I often find my thoughts going to a rather ugly place of jealousy. I know God has forgiven the sins of my past, yet I seem to frequently have such regrets and feel that God will, at some time, judge me for all of my wrong decisions."

"It is tough to get our minds wrapped around something like grace. Or, maybe more accurately, it is tough for us to let grace wrap itself around our minds."

The gals both laughed. Jodie continued, "You aren't the only one to have doubts, fears, and regrets. I, myself, have often had them. I am so thankful that Jason is there to remind me of grace and how the Holy Spirit works in our lives to conquer those thoughts and feelings."

"You are so lucky to have Jason. Oh, there I go again. I'm comparing my life to yours. Believe me, I am glad you have Jason. I hope that, sometime in my future, I will have someone like him. Don't get me wrong—I'm not looking right now. I don't think there are too many Jason types out there who would be interested in an almost nine-month pregnant lady."

"Wow! Do you realize what you just called yourself?"

"No. What?"

"A lady! I don't think I have ever heard you refer to yourself in that way."

"You're right. I don't think I have ever thought of myself that way before."

"Do you know what that is?"

"What?"

"That is God working in your life. You are beginning to see yourself more like God sees you." Jodie nodded as she affirmed her sister.

"You might be right. There are times that I can scarcely believe that I am me from the way I act and speak lately. I can't believe that God has been working on me for such a short time." Kristen got up to leave. "I need to go get some things finished up for my MBA team, and then I want to get over to the church. The coffee shop renovation is almost done, and supplies should start coming any day now."

"Do you want to come with me to see Elsa Hope again before you leave?"

"That would be great!"

Chapter 44

Kristen's schedule was a whirlwind as she completed her time with her MBA team, took finals, and worked on setting up Grounds of Hope. In her parents' attic, she had found some of her artwork from high school and decided that a few might look nice on the walls. She took them to Grounds for Hope and set them on the floor, spaced around the room. She arranged and rearranged them.

As she looked at the large wall across from the entry, she was suddenly reminded of some words from Isaiah 43. Pastor Ron had mentioned them in one of his recent talks, and Kristen pulled up the verses on her new Bible app. There they were—verses 18 and 19, "Forget the former things; do not dwell on the past. See I am doing a new thing! Now it springs up; do you not perceive it?" It would be great to have those verses across that wall. Even though she herself was rather artistic, calligraphy was not her strong suit. Almost immediately, she thought of Maureen from her high school art class. Calligraphy was her specialty. She had not been in contact with any of her high school classmates since she took off for New York City right after graduation. She wondered if Maureen was still in the city. Had she married and had a different last name now? She fought hard to try to remember her last name. It started with a C—something like Carson, but it wasn't Carson. Kristen closed her eyes and tried to recall the name. It just wouldn't come to her. "Oh!" she thought out loud. "My old yearbook is in the attic." She left the coffee shop in a hurry and dashed home to check.

She found it in the box labeled "Kristen's books." There it was, her old *Footprints*. She quickly found that Maureen's last name was Courison. There couldn't be too many Courisons in the area. She determined that she would find her, and find her, she did. Maureen's mom remembered Kristen. After Kristen assured them that she was no longer the impetuous senior she used to be, her mom said that Maureen was married and lived about twenty miles away. She was working as a receptionist in a dental office there. She even gave Kristen her daughter's phone number. Kristen gushed her gratitude. She couldn't call Maureen fast enough.

After exchanging some getting reacquainted pleasantries and reviewing what Kristen wanted for the coffee shop, Maureen agreed to meet her there the next afternoon.

As she took in the mocha-colored wall, Maureen said, "I was really surprised that you wanted a Bible verse on the wall of your coffee shop. If I remember correctly, your family was into that God thing, but you wanted to get far away from that."

"You are right. That was me. That is the main reason that I chose this verse. It talks about the past and reminds me not to dwell there. It reminds me that there are new things ahead."

"Well, I am not really a church person myself, but I do still love to do calligraphy. Do you have some paper? I can show you some different styles, and you can choose the one you like best."

She wrote several, including *"Forget the former things,"* "Forget the former things," and "Forget the former things."

Kristen decided she liked the first one the best. "It seems like it has a sense of elegance and yet shows a spirit of fun."

"That's the one I would choose as well," Maureen agreed. "Now, what color?"

"What do you think?"

"Your wall is such a nice, warm, dark mocha color. I am thinking a cream color would make it look like something you would like in your coffee cup." Maureen raised her eyebrows in a questioning way.

"Yeah." Kristen nodded her approval. "I like it."

"Okay, when would you want me to do it? Would Saturday morning work? My husband works on Saturday mornings, but we like to keep the rest of the weekend open so we can do things together."

"Saturday morning would be perfect!" Kristen's excitement shone in her eyes.

After Maureen left, it dawned on Kristen that she had not run this decision past Joyce. She quickly called Joyce and explained her plan. Joyce was thrilled with the design that Kristen described and asked if she could come by on Saturday to see the work in progress or the finished product.

Saturday morning dawned bright and clear. Kristen moved as fast as her swollen belly would allow. She rushed to the coffee shop, making sure to get there before Maureen arrived.

During the morning, the conversation turned to the purpose of the business. Kristen detailed her experiences from the time she left high school and right through her giving her life over to God. She then talked about her classes, the MBA team, the church leadership team, all the ways God had worked in her life, and how He had brought about this dream.

Talk moved on to Kristen's pregnancy. Maureen hesitantly revealed that her husband and she had been expecting a baby and had lost their little girl when she was about seven months along. "One day, I realized that I had not felt any kicks for a while. The hospital confirmed that there was no longer a heartbeat. They gave me some drugs to start delivery. The doctor said that our baby was not developing properly and that there was no way she would have survived. That is when I decided that, if there was a God, He didn't really care about me or our baby."

"Oh, I am so sorry." Kristen expressed her deep concern.

"What kind of God would do that to us—to our baby? Why us?" Maureen's jaw was set, but she blinked back tears, and her voice broke.

"I don't really know how to answer you. I am new to all of this myself. All I know is that God loves us all and that He wants to live in us." Kristen was feeling quite inadequate in her response.

"Well, until I can get a good answer to it, I am not going to be running to embrace any god."

"I can't say that I blame you," Kristen replied.

Maureen continued her work on the verse on the wall. Kristen was amazed at how fast she was able to form such beautiful letters. Every time Kristen looked up from her work, it looked better. She was so glad she had made this decision.

When Maureen was nearly finished, Joyce walked in. "I'll have a Columbian espresso." She smiled.

Kristen looked up. "Actually, by this time on Monday, I would be able to get one for you. I plan to make one of everything that will be on my menu—kind of a final check on my recipes, ingredients, supplies, and layout. It will also give me an idea of how long it takes to make each item.

"This looks great!" Joyce exclaimed.

"Maureen, this is Joyce. She and I have been meeting every week to keep this all on track."

Maureen greeted Joyce and smiled at her acknowledgment of Joyce's praise. "Oh, I wish that I had Monday off. I would come to be your taste-tester."

Maureen turned back to finish her work. In making her turn, her foot slipped on the rung, and she fell. Her paint jar and brush went flying, spraying paint all over what she had completed. "No, no, no!" she cried.

Both Joyce and Kristen rushed to her. "Are you okay?" they shouted at the same time.

"I am, but look at the wall. It's ruined!" Maureen cried. "I ruined it!"

"It was an accident," Kristen consoled her. "You didn't do it on purpose. What you did was beautiful."

"But it is not beautiful anymore." Maureen put her head into her hands.

The splotches and splatters of cream-colored paint completely covered parts of the writing. The three of them sat there for a while, staring at the wall. They all got up and started cleaning the paint from the floor and the ladder.

"Hey, I think I just got an inspiration," Kristen said, looking at the wall. "Yeah, I don't think it is ruined at all. I think you can make something really beautiful out of this mess."

"How?" Maureen questioned.

"What if we let it dry as it is and then you go back and re-write, in the mocha color, the letters that were destroyed? The writing would change from cream on mocha to mocha on cream." Kristen explained.

"I think that might work," Maureen said as she got up from the floor. "This will need a couple of hours to dry, and I really need to go meet Tristan."

Joyce looked at her.

"Tristan—my husband. We are going hiking this afternoon," Maureen clarified.

"We still have some time to complete it. You go. Joyce and I will finish cleaning up here," Kristen said thoughtfully.

"I could come back Tuesday evening if that would work."

"Perfect. We have our church leadership meeting that night, and they will be excited to see the progress and how close we are to opening." Kristen said, and Joyce nodded.

"Okay then—Tuesday after I get off work. I can be here around six. Let me get a quick picture of it before I go, so I know what I will be working on."

"See you then." Kristen and Joyce waved as Maureen left the shop.

Tuesday evening, Joyce and Kristen welcomed Maureen back to the shop. The wall had dried nicely, and the splatters had taken on an artistic appeal.

Grasping her paintbrush and the mocha paint, Maureen went to work on finishing her calligraphy. Kristen and Joyce went next door to meet with the leadership team.

Maureen was just adding the final "Isaiah 43:18 & 19" when the door opened. Kristen led a small procession into the coffee shop.

"Everyone, this is Maureen. She is the talent behind our focus wall."

Maureen turned to look at the group. She smiled and made a wave toward the wall. "This isn't exactly the way we had planned it, but it is working out."

"I'll say it is." Ted was the first to speak. "This reminds me of my own life. I had made a mess of things. I actually blamed God for my mess. When I finally turned my life over to Him, He took my mess and made it into something pretty fantastic."

"I think it would not have nearly the impact without the splatters," Pastor Ron added. "It does look like life."

Maureen's eyes widened as she listened to the comments about her work. Her thoughts were drawn to how she didn't want anything to do with a God who could mess things up.

She looked again at the wall. She read the words that she had painted there. Although she had read them many times while working on this project, she had an uncanny sense that she was reading them for the first time. New thoughts filled her mind. Could there be a God who actually did care for her and about her? Ted's words burrowed into her very soul.

"I actually blamed God for my mess." She wondered, *Have I been wrong to blame Him for the death of my unborn baby?* She turned away from the wall and said, "I'll be finished here in just a few more minutes."

Joyce smiled at her. "We don't want to hold up your work, but we just couldn't wait to show it to everyone."

"And we thank you for your contribution to Grounds of Hope," Ted interjected.

"It was my pleasure. I enjoyed doing it and reconnecting with an old high school friend." Maureen picked up her brush and turned back to her work.

"Thank you again!" Pastor Ron concluded as the team returned to the church side of the building, leaving Maureen alone with her painting and her thoughts.

Chapter 45

The WinterCare division of Igland Landscaping had been finally put to rest for the season. The landscaping projects now were well underway, with the large Tackner horse property taking shape. Jason found it refreshing to once again be able to drive and oversee the work his crew was doing. Even though he was currently unable to do any of the manual work, he could tell that the team seemed to work better when he was on site. He now met weekly with Matt, in hopes of getting the remodeling and renovation part of the business up and running.

Matt invited Jason to see the progress that was being made on his mother's kitchen. Jason was impressed with the transformation that had already taken place. The design gave the appearance of much more space, with the openness to the dining area and living room.

"How have you been able to get all of this done?" Jason asked. "You have done my Box Reno, been taking care of our WinterCare clients, and have been working every day since on the Tackner property, not to mention the time you have been putting in at the apartments."

Matt chuckled a bit. "I forgot to tell you. I never sleep."

"No. Really. I don't see how you could have done this much."

"Well, I learned from the best. When I was on my first job with you, I couldn't believe how much you could accomplish in a day." He ran his hand over the surface of the new island. "You do remember, don't you, that I don't have a wife—or any social life. I live right here at the job site, which makes it possible for me to work several hours in the evening and sometimes into the night."

"Oh, you just reminded me. I've been meaning to speak to you about that." Jason jabbed his friend and coworker. "About your social life."

"What about it? I happen to think it is suiting me just fine at the moment."

"You know, you are not getting any younger and—"

"Stop right there! You are beginning to sound like my mother. I think I have heard this talk at least every other week since I graduated from college," Matt stated. "If you are about to tell me that there is this really nice lady who would be perfect for me, you can just forget it."

"No, no, nothing like that. I won't say another word about it, except this—don't keep yourself so involved with work and your projects that you are not willing to see what else God might have for you."

"I have pretty much thought that God knows where I am, and He knows what I need. Right now, He has given me work to do and this kitchen to complete. I figure that, if He thinks I need a woman in my life, He will send her along." Matt turned to face Jason. "But to be perfectly honest, I do think about my future, and I would hope that it will include a wife and children. You must know how much I admire the relationship that you have with Jodie—and especially now, with your baby girl."

"I am very blessed to have Jodie and Elsa Hope in my life," Jason agreed. "I can't picture my life any other way. I will be so glad when we get to bring her home and begin to live as a family."

"Do you have any idea yet how long that will be?"

"Soon, they say. She is such a strong little person. She has been gaining weight well. Each day, she is making noticeable progress. Jodie thinks that she may get to come home next weekend." Jason's broad grin conveyed his joy.

"Okay. I guess that means I should prepare to lead the crew next week."

"I guess it does. Is there anything you need?" Jason asked.

"No, I think we are fine." Matt squared his shoulders and looked at his boss. "Last fall gave me the experience I needed in getting the crew to work together. And Phil—he has really stepped up to the plate, even when you are not there."

"Then, assuming that my little girl gets to come home, I will count on you taking the reins again for at least one week."

"That will be great, except you do know that having a newborn at home will mean that your sleep may be a bit more interrupted. At least that's what they say." Matt laughed.

"Oh, I know that, but it will be worth it. If it gets too bad, I guess I could come over here and help the guy who never sleeps."

"And your sister-in-law, Kristen—she must be about to have her baby too," Matt said.

"She is. I think her due date is just a week or so away. Her coffee shop is about ready to open as well. I don't know which will come first—the baby or the grand opening."

"That whole coffee shop thing has really gone fast. It was great getting to sample her baking and soups when she was fine-tuning her recipes." Matt could almost taste again the delicious scones and the tasty soups that she had brought to the crew.

"You know, Kristen is planning a family evening at the shop next Monday. Since we don't know if Elsa Hope is coming home this weekend, I am not sure we will be going. I am thinking that Kristen wouldn't mind if you came, especially since you have been putting so much time into the apartments. She wants to have us all help her decide on a few of the menu items and see how the shop would run with actual customers ordering." Jason ran his hand through his hair. "And you are close enough to be family, and I know Kristen considers you a friend." Their conversation was interrupted by Jason's phone. He stepped around the corner to speak, far enough to afford some privacy, yet it was not far enough that Matt could not hear Jason's part of the conversation.

"Hi, sweetheart."

"Really!"

"That soon?"

"What do I need to do?"

"This is beyond what we had hoped!"

"Okay! I will see you in about an hour."

"Love you so much!"

"You too."

"Bye-bye!"

With a spring in his step, he moved back into the room, "Sorry, Matt, I have to run. Jodie said that the doctor is planning to release Elsa Hope on Sunday."

"No problem! I am very happy for you. Oh, and, Jason, get some sleep tonight."

"I will." Jason smiled as he went out the door. "At least we will try to."

Matt returned to his work on the kitchen with renewed vigor. He had never been the jealous sort. He had always enjoyed finding contentment in his life. Recently, though, he had found himself thinking of what it might be like to have what Jason had—a wife, a baby, a family. He was increasingly aware that there was a place in his heart that longed for those relationships. He closed his eyes for a moment and told God that he trusted Him to direct his life.

Matt's mother was thrilled with the way her new kitchen was nearing completion. Almost every day, she was taking pictures of the process and the progress. Matt realized that these pictures might actually become useful as an advertising portfolio of his renovation work.

As if he did not have enough irons in the fire, Matt enrolled in a six-week online small business accounting class. He was grateful that there were no set hours, and he often found himself listening to the lectures and doing his assignments at some very unusual times. He could see how this information was going to be useful in both the landscaping and renovation parts of the business.

Chapter 46

Tiny Elsa Hope Igland was welcomed home on Sunday afternoon. Never had Jodie and Jason felt such joy entering their home. Their family was complete, or at least as complete as it would be for now. They took many pictures to record the firsts—the first time in the car seat, the first car ride, the first time through the door, the first time on the couch, and the first time in the crib.

"What a wonderful adventure we have begun," Jodie remarked as they stood by the crib, watching their baby sleep.

Jason wrapped his arm around his wife's waist, and she responded by putting her arm around him and laying her head on his shoulder. "I feel like I want to stand here next to her forever."

Jason gave her a squeeze and said, "You say that right now, but I think that it won't be long before you want her to take her nap so you can get things done or get a few moments of rest yourself."

"I know they always say that new moms should rest when the baby is resting. She is just so sweet that I don't want to miss anything."

"Let's go and let her sleep. The baby monitor is on so we can hear her when she stirs." Jason took Jodie's hand and led her out of the room.

They had invited her parents and Kristen over for a light dinner. In all reality, they invited them, but the three insisted that they would bring the light dinner. Shortly after five, they arrived, and the family's welcome home celebration began.

Kristen had made her own croissants and her special chicken salad with cranberries. Her first shipment of the boutique kettle-fried chips had arrived at the shop, so Kristen brought some of those and a few unique kosher dills to complement the sandwiches. Bonnie had ordered a decorated cake for dessert. Everyone marveled at the likeness of Elsa Hope on the cake with "Welcome Home" written in pink and ribbon of dainty pink frosting rosebuds.

Elsa Hope awakened as everyone trooped into the nursery. Jodie lifted her dolly from the crib and laid her on the changing table. "Let me put a fresh diaper on her, and then we can start passing her around."

Grandma Bonnie got first honors to hold her granddaughter. She could not help snuggling her in close and smothering her head with kisses.

"Kristen," Dale remarked, "I think you are going to have some loyal customers when you open. This has got to be about the best sandwich that I have ever had. I can't wait to sample the full menu."

"You know you won't have to wait long, Dad. I can't wait to have you all there tomorrow to taste my offerings." Kristen took a bite of her own croissant sandwich and smiled broadly. "It is good, isn't it!" She beamed.

Everyone agreed that the sandwiches were delicious, as were the pickles and chips.

"I know that this is to be a rather small deal tomorrow night, but I invited Matt to come," admitted Jason. "I hope that's okay. I should have asked you first."

"Oh, that's fine. I also invited Joyce and her husband and Maureen and Tristan," Kristen said. "I can't believe that we are getting this close to opening." She stopped for a minute and then continued. "My MBA team suggested that I open quietly and run for about a week before I advertise a grand opening event."

"Why's that?" Bonnie asked.

"It's so I can get used to running the shop before we are inundated by people who want to attend a grand opening. I can get my crew acclimated to the workflow."

"So when do you think you might be doing the quiet opening?" Dale inquired.

"There are so many moving parts to all of this. I have talked with a girl I met through Joyce, and she has some experience in running a similar shop. She is also pregnant, and the baby's father is not involved with her anymore—kind of like me. She is very interested in coming to work with me. I will need to rely heavily on her when my little guy is born. She would be in charge while I was out—I guess she would be my Matt.

"Of course, the apartments are not going to be ready for another month, but she has somewhere to stay right now. And her baby isn't due for another three months." Kristen reached out to take her turn at spoiling her niece. Elsa Hope settled comfortably into her arms. "I am planning to have three or four people working at a time. I went to the college group from church the other night, and there were about six or seven who said that they would like to donate some hours each week."

"I like the sound of that—young people who are willing to give of themselves without expecting a big monetary reward." Dale nodded. "If I remember correctly, you are planning to operate from six a.m. to three p.m. Is that correct?"

"Yes, at least at the start. And we will only operate Mondays through Saturdays. I am planning that those who work the entire day would have three half-hour breaks. That way, we can each keep a close eye on our own baby and each other's babies." Kristen let out a deep sigh. "There are still several details that need to be worked out—like hiring another full-time person."

Elsa Hope began to squirm, and Kristen adjusted her hold on the baby. Not satisfied, her niece began to cry. "I think she needs her momma." Kristen frowned as she held the baby out to her sister.

"I suspect she is hungry. It has been nearly two hours." Jodie took her little girl and headed for the living room. "Keep talking. I can hear you from here, and I want to hear all the plans."

"Of course, you do!" Kristen laughed. "You want to make sure I have considered everything that you would have put on a spreadsheet."

"Maybe a little bit," Jodie admitted. "But mostly, I just want to be in the know. Do you have your quiet opening day in mind?"

"It's actually called a soft opening. I know it is risky, and I talked it over with Joyce, but we are thinking about opening a week from tomorrow and having the grand opening the following Monday. We talked about how I could possibly miss my own grand opening. I'm hoping that this little guy will wait until that is over."

Bonnie looked at her daughter. "Would you be okay with that? Missing it?"

"I think it will be okay. The alternative would be that we don't open for another month or so, and I certainly don't want to wait that long. I think it would actually be harder to have a grand opening while caring for a newborn."

"I think you are making the right decision," her dad said. "The leadership team is behind this project, and they will be encouraged to see that it is moving forward. I wouldn't be a bit surprised that other church people would volunteer to help if you were not able to be there."

The whole family seemed to breathe a collective sigh of relief.

"Okay," Jason said. "Ready or not, here we go!"

Everyone nodded and chuckled with excitement.

Jodie returned to the table with her sleeping daughter. "So, Kristen, are there any last-minute details that I could help with? Now that I am not going to the hospital every day, I probably could help out."

"Just be careful that you do not overdo, Jodie," Bonnie reminded her.

"I won't, Mom. Remember, I have had time to recover from the delivery. I think that having my schedule chiseled down to just caring for Elsa Hope here at home will seem like a breeze. I just want to be a small part of this endeavor."

"I like it." Kristen nodded to her sister. "Let's get together tomorrow morning, and you can make a spreadsheet for me of all the details that still need to be decided and of all the work that still needs to be done. I think I can use some more of your organizational skills at this point."

"Yeah!" Jodie giggled. "And it is never too early to introduce Elsa Hope to spreadsheets."

Chapter 47

Kristen and Jodie spent the morning together, putting onto the spreadsheet every bit of minutia that had to do with the opening and smooth operating of Grounds for Hope. What had once been a point of contention between the sisters now had become a cornerstone of cooperation. Convinced that they had exhausted all the possible tasks to be done and decisions yet to be made, they printed the sheets. Kristen gathered them up and left for the coffee shop. Jodie had promised her that she would get some rest that afternoon.

At the shop, Kristen set to work, baking scones and brownies, preparing two of her soups, chopping fresh vegetables, and making sure that the utensils and containers were in their proper places. Her deli meats were ready to be sliced, and everything was ready to go. She placed a call to Susan, the pregnant woman who knew Joyce, and confirmed that she wanted to be a part of the Grounds for Hope team. Susan asked about the apartments and indicated that eventually she would like to live there. She agreed to work Friday afternoon with Kristen so she could learn the menu and how to make the brownies and other baked items. Kristen decided that, for now, she alone would make her specialty scones. She was not ready to disclose her secret recipe, especially not to someone she had not yet met. She did not know what she would do once her baby was born. She might then need to let someone else bake them for a time. Of course, they would be sworn to secrecy. Another option would be that, while she was out, the shop just would not have scones. It just might make them even more special.

She checked the spreadsheets that Jodie had prepared for her. She made checkmarks next to the items she completed today. Tomorrow, she would concentrate on personnel. She still needed to find one more person to work nearly full-time and schedule her to train with Susan on Friday. She also had to firm up schedules for the college students. She planned to train them on Saturday. And then there was that personnel software that the MBA team had made available. It would keep track of the hours, the rate of pay, the Social Security payments, and it would even issue checks. She would need to spend some time getting the staff set up on that. Wednesday would be devoted to promotion. She needed to get something for the church bulletin about the grand opening and some "Coming Soon" posters to be placed in the church lobby. Those who came to community classes and events at the building would be informed of the soft opening as well as the grand opening. Thursday was the final day to order perishables for the next week. She was confident that she had this part well in hand. After all, she had already done her personal run-through and had gotten everything ready for tonight. Thursday was to be her breather day before the training days, but it was also the day that the food inspector was coming for the initial inspection. Kristen was not worried about that since she had spent much time studying the regulations, and at Pete's, she had been the one to oversee all the compliance issues.

Kristen greeted her first customers as her parents arrived at the shop. They were followed by Maureen and Tristan. Matt was the next to arrive. The Iglands, arriving with bag and baby carrier, were a little late.

"I can't believe we are late!" Jodie exclaimed. "I don't think I have ever been late in my life. Who knew that such a little person could have such a massive impact on our time schedule!"

Everyone laughed.

Maureen came in close to see the new baby. "Isn't she beautiful? Tristan, come and see!"

Tristan shrugged his shoulders and gave in to his wife's request. He nodded as he looked at the sleeping baby. "Yep, it's a baby all right! And, yes, she is very pretty." He shook Jason's hand. "Congratulations to you! I am Tristan."

"Jason," the baby's father replied in way of introduction. "And this is Elsa Hope and my wife, Jodie."

"Pleased to meet you. I am glad your sister-in-law invited us to this event."

"I think you are in for a treat. Kristen certainly knows her way around a kitchen, and she has developed some right tasty soups and sandwiches." Jason licked his lips to emphasize his point.

"I can't wait to try them," Tristan replied. Turning back toward Maureen, he pointed at the wall opposite them. "That's it? That's the wall you did?"

"Uh-huh."

"It does look good. When you told me about it and the accident, I could not imagine that it could look like this."

Maureen smiled at her husband. He continued, "It actually looks like it had been planned this way from the start."

Kristen took the orders from each of her guests. Although her mom offered to help, Kristen declined, insisting that she needed to be able to do this by herself. Jodie had suggested that she use a timer tonight so she would have a better idea of how long it would take her to serve a customer. She agreed that it would be a good idea, and she found herself glancing periodically at the timer. She did not want to run herself ragged—not that she could run much at all being so close to her due date—but she did want to mimic the serving of real customers. She found that she was able to serve them all quite efficiently. She made mental note of a few changes she would make in the layout of utensils and supplies.

While her guests were enjoying their meals, Kristen cleaned the kitchen area. She then came and sat down with them. She had prepared a sandwich and a bowl of soup for herself. She was pleased as she sampled her creations.

All agreed that the soups and sandwiches were beyond delicious. Kristen convinced everyone to have a brownie. Again, her baking received rave reviews. Jodie asked her how the timing went, and Kristen replied that she was pleased with her time management. At least she had done well serving her very small clientele.

"If we can keep up the pace I had tonight, we should be good. I think we can do that since there will be at least three of us instead of one."

Before everyone left, Maureen pulled a large roll from her bag and handed it to Kristen. "Here, this is a shop-warming present," she said.

Kristen eyed her in wonderment as she began to unroll the piece.

"Look, everyone!" she squealed. "It's a grand opening banner!"

"I'll add the day and date when you let me know," Maureen offered.

"That's beautiful!" Jodie chimed in. "Maureen, you do very, very nice work. I bet you could do this full-time."

"I love the steaming cup of coffee on it," Kristen commented.

"And the printing is so nice—what do you call it? Calliphony? Calliraddy?" her dad teased.

"Calligraphy, Dad!" Kristen rolled her eyes as she had often done as a teen.

Dale grinned as he gave a playful punch to his daughter's arm.

Maureen gathered up her things and headed toward the door. She suddenly stopped and turned toward Kristen. "Do you think you might have a few minutes tomorrow? Maybe we could meet for lunch?"

"I think that would be great."

"Could you meet me at Stefano's for their lunch buffet? Say around twelve thirty?" Maureen's face looked rather serious.

"I'll see you then," Kristen replied with raised eyebrows.

After everyone except her parents had left, the three sat together at a table.

"Can you believe it?" Kristen exclaimed with a sweeping of her hand toward the shop.

Bonnie smiled and nodded. "This has truly been a miracle. I can scarcely believe how fast this has all come together."

"I know! Who would have thought a year ago that a girl who was running as hard as she could away from God would be sitting here about to open a coffee shop that was prayed into existence." Kristen looked around the shop and breathed in deeply. "As much as Grounds for Hope is a miracle, I still think the larger miracle is me."

"I agree," her dad said as he placed an arm around his daughter.

"Well, I am getting tired. I'll get things all cleaned up here, and then I'll be home," Kristen said, getting up from the table.

"Tell you what." Her mother smiled. "Let the two of us help you with the cleaning, and we will all get to bed sooner."

Chapter 48

Kristen and Maureen arrived at Stefano's at almost the same time. They filled their plates with a sampling of salads and entree creations inspired by Joe's native Italy. From the refreshing antipasto to his specialty meatballs and freshly made pasta, everything was served with a huge helping of authenticity. Nobody did an Italian lunch buffet like Joe Stefano.

As they savored the enchanting flavors of their selections, their conversation suddenly became more serious.

"Kristen," Maureen began, "I wanted to have lunch with you today because I am glad that we have reconnected, but the main reason is that I wanted to talk with you about the change in you. I think I might want to have that change in my own life."

"Wow! I wasn't expecting that!" Kristen responded. "What do you want to know?"

"Well, as I told you, we've been pretty mad at God. I wasn't even sure that He existed, you know, because of the death of my baby. But lately, ever since the paint accident, it seems like thoughts of God keep popping into my mind."

"I think I know what you mean." Kristen nodded. "I remember that happening to me. It was like I couldn't get away from the thoughts. It seemed like they were chasing me everywhere."

"How did you finally make the change? I mean, there must have been some point in time when you gave in to the thoughts."

"Yes, there was." Kristen toyed with a piece of mozzarella in her caprese. "That point for me was Christmas Eve at the candlelight service at Valley Edge."

Kristen then explained how through that service, she had come to that point of giving herself to God. Maureen listened carefully, thinking deeply about her own life. "Was it hard for you to do that? Have you ever second-guessed that decision?"

"It was hard only because I had been so opposed to anything that had to do with God and religion. I thought that there was no way that God would even want me. I thought that He would always be upset for the way that I had messed things up."

"I am thinking that I want to do that, but I don't know when I will be able to get to a church to do it." Maureen swallowed, and her eyes brimmed with moisture.

"That is one thing I have learned about God. He doesn't require us to come to a certain place. He meets us—no matter where we are. He just asks us to open our empty hearts and let Him fill them. Does that make any sense?" Kristen reached across the table and took Maureen's hand in her own.

"You mean, I could do that right here? In Stefano's? This doesn't seem like a very religious place."

"All my life, I had been looking at religion and seeing all its shortcomings, and I realized, finally, that I didn't need religion, but I did need a relationship with God. I discovered that God wanted the same with me." Kristen paused a bit and then continued, "Listen, I am not really experienced in this myself. All I know is what God has done for me since I gave control of my life over to Him."

"I see the huge change in you, Kristen, and that is the change I want for myself. How do I do it?"

Kristen told Maureen again what she did that night in December. The two of them bowed their heads as the truth of what God had done through His Son's death sank deep into Maureen's heart.

Before they got into their cars, Maureen hugged Kristen and said, "I am not sure how I am going to explain all of this to Tristan, but I will find a way. I think he might have a suspicion that I have been thinking about all of this. I know he will be surprised that I am ready to let go of the bitter hurt I was carrying in my heart."

Chapter 49

After she had gotten up for the third time that morning, Jodie called her sister. She convinced Kristen to come to her house to work on her goal for the day—employees.

Kristen arrived with leftover scones and soup in hand. "I need to have these eaten before they go stale."

"I would never turn down this," her sister greeted her. "Elsa Hope is down for another nap. I have to take my breaks when I get them."

"Well, I guess then I will have to wait a bit for my chance to love on my niece. I know preemies have a shorter time between feedings and take shorter naps. That must be very wearing on you."

"I think I am getting more used to the schedule—such as it is"—Jodie gestured with her hands—"I have to get little cat naps myself."

"So shouldn't you be resting now?"

"No, I also need some adult interaction and sister time." Jodie changed the subject. "How are you coming with your plan for the week?"

"Right on schedule, so far." Kristen pulled her spreadsheets from her bag. "See, I have actually been checking off each item as it is accomplished."

Jodie perused the papers that her sister placed in front of her. She smiled when she noticed that Kristen had already messaged all the college kids who had indicated that they wanted to participate in Grounds for Hope.

"Right here is where I have marked those who have confirmed and the days and hours they are available." Kristen pointed out the various columns. "I still need to find another almost full-time person."

"I might know of someone. There was a preemie baby born shortly before Elsa Hope was released. The mom was about twenty-five and not married. She was very worried about how she was going to raise her son by herself. Her mother had told her that she could not bring her baby home to her house because there just wasn't not any more room. She had been in contact with some homeless shelters, but she didn't want her son to start his life that way. She seemed like she was motivated to bettering her life. Would you like for me to try to contact her?"

"Do you know her name?"

"Just Maddie—no wait—it was on her son's incubator. What was it?" Jodie screwed up her face as she tried hard to think of the last name that was posted there. She shook her head. "No, I can't think of it."

"So you have a first name. How will you find her? Are you going to contact the homeless shelters and ask if Maddie is there? Like they'd tell you even if they did."

"No, I think I know right where to find her. This afternoon, I will take Elsa Hope and go to the hospital. I am sure her son is still there. I will just wait there until she shows up." Jodie tapped the open slot on Kristen's spreadsheet. I might just be able to fill that slot for you.

Kristen penciled "Maddie" in the empty cell. "But the apartments aren't ready yet. How would she be able to juggle a newborn preemie and a job from a homeless shelter?" Kristen looked at her sister.

"I am not sure, but if it is meant to be, God will make a way."

The sisters spent the rest of the morning poring over the spreadsheets and fitting the "I'm available" responses into the openings. Kristen figured that she should aim for overstaffing the first month or so.

"Remember, you will need to be taking off some time when your own little one makes his appearance." Jodie looked over the schedules again.

"I have already considered that, and I am thinking that I will take two to three weeks, although I will be checking in on a daily basis." Kristen rubbed her hand over her bulging belly.

"It's too bad that your delivery date and the opening are going to be so close together. The business will be just getting started, and there will sure to be some unanticipated bumps." Jodie reached over and patted her sister's abdomen.

"I wish I had a Matt like Jason has—someone who knew the business as well as he did." Kristen smiled to herself as she reflected on her words. *I wish I had a Matt.*

"When you train your college kids and Susan, you will probably find one who stands out. That person may well become your Matt."

"Susan does appear promising," Kristen said thoughtfully. "And it is good that she is not due for several months."

That afternoon, Jodie bundled up her precious daughter and made her way through the medical center. Finding a bench outside the NICU, she arranged her nest. Elsa Hope slept in her car seat beside her.

It was less than a half hour before Jodie spotted Maddie coming out of the NICU. Concern clouded the new mother's face.

"Maddie?" Jodie stopped her.

Startled, Maddie looked at Jodie, "Oh—uh, I'm sorry. I can't remember your name."

"It's Jodie."

"What are you doing back here? There is nothing wrong with your baby, is there?"

"No, no, she's fine. What about yours?"

"He has had a rough week. He seems to be getting better, but they told me this morning that he will be here for at least another three to four weeks—possibly longer." Maddie wiped a tear with the back of her hand.

"I know it is hard to wait, and babies seem so fragile when they are in the NICU. He will get stronger and bigger, and then you will have him home with you."

"Yeah! Home—wherever that will be."

"Your mother is still insisting that you move out?" Jodie asked.

"Yes. In fact, she told me that I can have three more weeks there. I have not found any place to go, and I really don't want to bring Geoffrey home to a shelter." Maddie shook her head and dropped her gaze.

"Do you have a few minutes to sit and talk?" Jodie motioned to the bench as she moved the sleeping Elsa Hope to the floor.

"Sure. I have nowhere to go. Literally!"

Jodie explained the soon-to-be-opened Grounds for Hope and her sister's need for another full-time-ish person. She told of the apartments with the expected completion in another few weeks. As Jodie described the opportunity and the purpose of the coffee shop, Maddie's face began to brighten.

"This might work," Maddie said slowly and carefully. "If Geoffrey doesn't get to come home for another four weeks, I could maybe move right into an apartment! I could have a home for him. I could have a job. We could have a future."

"There are some requirements for living in the apartments, and you would have to sign off on those. You don't do drugs or have an alcohol problem?"

"No—nothing like that. I don't smoke either, in case that is another restriction. I just made some bad choices in my personal life."

"So you are interested?"

"Yes, definitely. I haven't worked in a coffee shop before, but I have some experience with fast food."

"Let's exchange contact information, and my sister will be talking with you soon. In fact, it will be very soon, as she hopes to have all the staff lined up by tonight or tomorrow. Maddie, what is your last name?"

"Bainwright. Maddie Bainwright."

"I'm Jodie Igland. My sister is Kristen Petersen."

Elsa Hope began to squirm, and Jodie reached to pick her up. "Would you like to hold her for a bit? I know she will be hungry, but I remember what it was like wondering if I'd ever get to hold my own baby for more than a few moments at a time." Jodie held her baby out toward to Maddie.

Maddie smiled as she held the baby in her arms. "She seems so big! I guess she is compared to Geoffrey, that is."

"That is a term that I hadn't heard yet in reference to Elsa Hope—big." Jodie chuckled. "But you are right. She is a lot bigger than she was when she was here. She has just topped six pounds."

Maddie handed the baby back to her mother and got up to leave. "I look forward to hearing from your sister. I hope this works out for all of us."

"Me too," Jodie responded. "I'll be praying for you and Geoffrey."

"Thank you very much! It can't hurt—and who knows? It might help."

Chapter 50

Kristen couldn't believe how fast the days were passing. She had her staff in place, and her Friday training with Maddie and Susan went amazingly well. The way that Susan handled herself in the kitchen and proved her knowledge and skills gave Kristen confidence in her ability to run the shop. Maddie, while having no former barista experience, proved herself a quick study. She picked up on the terms and moved efficiently around the shop. She left after two hours so she could be at the hospital with her son. Kristen was pleased to see her return promptly at 2:00 p.m. for a few more hours of training. Saturday morning brought the rest of the staff, all eager to learn their trade, however temporary it might be. Most of them had finished their finals and said that they might be able to work even more than they had originally indicated—at least for the summer. Kristen impressed on them that they should take any other summer employment opportunities that came to them and that she would work around their schedules. Each staff member reviewed the schedule for the coming week. They discussed the flexibility that would be needed when Kristen would deliver and Maddie's need to be at the hospital with her baby. Everyone agreed to pick up the empty spaces that would result from those events. Since all her staff were working a minimum wage or were volunteering their hours, Kristen encouraged them to have soup, sandwiches, and coffee on the house.

Before the Saturday training ended, the team gathered in front of the wall. Kristen thanked each of them for their commitment to this endeavor. She asked that they read together the verses on the wall, Isaiah 43:18 and 19, "Forget the former things; do not dwell on the past. See I am doing a new thing! Now it springs up; do you not perceive it?" Kristen looked around at the individuals who stood before her. "I can hardly believe that we are on the threshold of this new venture. It is totally a work of God—we must always remember that this belongs to Him."

James, one of the college kids, suggested that they put their hands together like an athletic team and have a cheer of "It all belongs to God!" Everyone agreed as each put a hand into the circle. "It all belongs to God!" bounced off the walls and the ceiling.

Kristen invited them all outside to the front of the shop. She carried the grand opening sign, now complete with the date and time. Together, they each took a turn at pounding the stakes into the ground. "It's official," Kristen announced. "We are opening a coffee shop."

"We need a picture," Susan said. "The founding staff. Who knows when we will all be together again?"

After posing for the photo, everyone said their goodbyes and left, prepared for the soft opening on Monday.

Very early Monday morning, Kristen was at Grounds of Hope, busily preparing the scones, muffins, and croissants that would be served that day. Maddie showed up to prep the romaine, spinach, and vegetables for the salads and sandwiches. She smiled as she placed the clear containers, each sporting a label with the contents, along with the date and time, in the refrigerator. The baked goods were soon in place on their trays in the display case. Kristen stepped in front of the case and scanned the display. She was pleased with the way everything looked, just waiting for the customers who would enjoy the delicious flavors. She whispered, "It all belongs to God." A funny thought hit her, and she chuckled out loud. "God, these are all Yours. Would You like one now?" Maddie overhead her spoken thought and laughed.

Another of the part-time staff, Krystle, arrived at 5:45. Krystle was a quiet person but very pleasant. She tied her Grounds of Hope apron and took her place behind the counter. At 6:00 a.m., the doors were unlocked, and the three looked at each other. "Showtime!" Maddie announced.

It was only a few minutes later that a couple from the church came in for coffee. "Are we the first?" the woman asked.

"Indeed, you are!" Kristen pulled her cell phone from her apron pocket. "Please place your order, and then, if it is okay with you, I would like to take your picture. You know this is history in the making, and it needs to be captured for posterity."

"Of course!" she replied. Turning to her husband, she said, "Isn't this a great little shop? What shall we get?"

The morning brought in a steady, light stream of customers. This was just how Kristen had hoped it would be. Krystle proved to be more outgoing than expected. She had a ready smile and greeting for each of the customers. When not taking orders, she took the initiative to clean tables and kept the shop ready for hungry and thirsty patrons. People started taking advantage of the outdoor seating once the sun had warmed the day. Susan arrived at eight to take Maddie's place. Cameron came at ten to complete the crew that would finish their first day of business. At 3:00 p.m., they locked the door and sat down together.

"This is scary," Kristen began.

"What do you mean? I thought it went very well," said Cameron.

"That's what scares me," replied Kristen. "It almost went too well. I am thinking that with this great of a soft opening, we may be in for a rough grand opening."

Krystle laughed out loud. "I would have never counted you in with the superstitious! I think that this great start is only evidence of how well you planned and how much God is blessing."

"I hope you are right. Let's clean her up and plan for a new day tomorrow."

"Who is coming in at six tomorrow?" Susan inquired.

Kristen pulled out her phone and checked her calendar. "That would be James—he will be here from five forty-five until ten. Maddie will come in again at five thirty and will stay until eight, when you will replace her. Then Ellie and Cameron will be in at ten."

Cameron nodded his agreement.

"And I will be back Saturday morning at six," Krystle chimed in. She was clearly enthused about the ministry.

Cameron asked, "Do you think we could have a two-week schedule posted in the break room? And maybe a place that we can access it online?"

"Those are both good ideas. I can get the paper one posted tomorrow. It will take me a while longer to figure out how to do one that you can access online."

"Oh, I think I can help you with that," he offered.

After relating the day's happenings to her parents and taking a refreshing shower, Kristen climbed into bed. She had intended to get right to sleep, but as soon as she shut her eyes, she opened them again. She could see her Bible on the nightstand, and she knew she should spend some time reading it. As she lay there, she spent some time arguing back and forth in her mind. "I really need my rest for tomorrow, but it was God who made today so great, and I need to hear from His Word."

She remembered a discussion that she had had with her dad several months ago. "Kristen," he had said, "God doesn't keep score, and He doesn't have a checklist of things that we need to do to get His blessing in our lives."

"That's it!" she realized. "Reading my Bible is not something that I have to do or even something that I should do. It is something that I want to do because I want to learn more of what God has for me."

With that, she picked up her Bible and started reading where she had left off in the book of Colossians. The seventeenth verse of the third chapter jumped out at her, "And whatever you do, whether in word or deed, do it all in the name of the Lord Jesus, giving thanks to God the Father through Him."

After spending some time mulling over these words, she thanked her Father for what He had done and gave the next day over to Him.

Chapter 51

Work progressed steadily on the apartments as Matthew, taking the lead, worked late almost every night, even after putting in a full day of landscaping with Jason. Excitement for the new coffee shop and the associated ministry ran high at the church. The grand opening sign was up, and business increased each day. As Kristen reviewed the financials, she could see that the coffee shop was already bringing in almost enough to cover the wages, consumables, and food supplies. The coming months would prove whether the business could sustain itself long-term.

On his drive home from the Tackner stable, Jason reflected on the past year. What a difference from the time when it was only Jodie and him. They would often spend a quiet Sunday lunch and afternoon with his parents-in-law. Kristen had been essentially estranged from the family, a burden that was heavy on all their hearts. Now their little family included Elsa Hope. Kristen, soon to have her own baby, was back in the family activities, and Sunday afternoons were seldom quiet. He contemplated his own journey through the accident, the surgeries, and the long recovery. He was relieved that the next surgery was to be the last. His activity level was getting close to what he would consider normal, although his surgeon cautioned him to continue to give his body the opportunity to fully heal. This, he had said, would take at least another six months. He could live with that. He remembered the St. Lucia breakfast that was reinstituted in the Peterson family. He recalled the wonderful Christmas where not only Kristen gave her life over to God, but he was able to surprise his wife with The Box renovation. Then there was the afternoon of delivering a bit of Christmas hope to the homeless, which was totally Kristen's idea.

He thought about the expansion of his business with taking in Matt as a partner. *Matt—how did I ever end up with him?* he thought. Matt's work ethic, his enthusiasm, and his commitment to his faith all came together to make him a great friend and business partner. He parked his truck in the driveway and gathered his lunch box and the other items that had accumulated on the floorboard.

Before he opened the front door, Jason's senses were alerted as he detected a delicious aroma. Jodie had certainly planned a great dinner. He eagerly anticipated sitting down to the table with his wife and with Elsa Hope in her little bouncy seat. Jodie always had her join them for dinner even if she slept the entire time.

Jodie met him at the door with a kiss. "Welcome home, love. Did you have a good day?"

"I did! And I can't wait to eat whatever smells so wonderful."

"I made a new recipe. It's sweet and sour meatloaf, but you are going to have to wait a bit. We are not having it here."

"No?"

Jodie shook her head. "No, we are meeting Mom and Dad and Kristen at the apartments. We know Matt has been putting in long hours there, and we are surprising him with a homemade dinner."

"That will be nice. He has been working so hard, trying to get the first two apartments done before Kristen has her baby and before Maddie's baby comes home." Jason took his lunch box to the kitchen and put his bag by the recliner. "I want to get cleaned up before we go. I will only be a few minutes." He stooped to place a soft kiss on his sleeping daughter's head and headed upstairs. He remembered that he used to take these steps two at a time. *That time will come again*, he vowed in his mind. *I guess maybe I do need another six months of recovery.*

Dale, Bonnie, and Kristen rode together to the soon-to-be Living Hope apartments. After she had left the shop, Kristen had made a mandarin orange almond flour cake. She was grateful that Susan had closed for her. She welcomed having a few more hours for herself, but, so like her, she had used that time to test a new recipe.

They could hear the pounding of Matt's hammer inside the apartment. Dale opened the door and hollered, "Hey, Matt! Do you have a moment to spare?"

Matt turned and saw Kristen with her cake. "I certainly have a moment to spare—especially when it involves one of Kristen's baked creations." He smiled broadly. "Is it something new?"

Kristen returned the smile. "Yes, it is a mandarin orange cake made with almond flour. If it is good, I will add to it our gluten-free selections at Grounds for Hope."

"I am sure it will be great. I have yet to sample something you made that was not delicious. You certainly do have a gift for baking."

Dale looked around the apartment, now near completion. "This has really come together nicely, Matt."

Matt smiled again. Kristen could not help but stare at his smile; it was so warm and genuine. She remembered her days in New York when she had plastered a smile on her face—a smile that was entirely fake, designed only to try to get someone to buy whatever she was selling. Matt's smile was nothing like that. His came from his very soul. It reached out to everyone around and drew smiles in return.

"Yeah, we're almost there, at least with the first two. Let me give you the grand tour." Matt motioned toward the kitchen. The kitchen appeared to be complete. The tile floor and the solid counter went together perfectly. The kitchen was small, but the way it was designed made a very adequate space in which to work. The appliances, although not top of the line, were stainless steel.

"Oh, this is beautiful," Kristen gushed. "I could see myself living here. I really like the little dining area. There is enough space to even have a few guests. And, oh, I love this backsplash. Is it glass?"

"Yes, it's glass tiles. I thought it worked well with the countertop."

Dale ran his hand over the counter. "What is this? It's not granite."

"No," Matt replied. "It is actually poured concrete."

"You're kidding!"

"Not kidding. It's amazing how these concrete tops can be made to look high-end."

"Well, I like it," Dale said. "You have done a fine job."

Kristen had already made her way up the stairs and peeked inside the bathroom, "Matt! This is lovely!" she hollered down the stairs.

"Glad you like it!" He grinned. "I tried to get it right. You know—a toilet, a sink, a shower, and a tub."

"It is so much more than that. And it has so much room." She spotted the linen closet behind the door. "What is this?" Before Matt could answer, she made the discovery herself. "It is a cabinet for a clothes hamper with a swinging door on top that looks like a drawer. This is genius!"

She turned from the bathroom and opened the door to the right of it. "It's a laundry room, with extra cabinet and shelving space! I was not expecting this!"

"The washer and dryer will be delivered tomorrow." Matt and Dale joined Kristen upstairs. "The warehouse bones of this building did not allow for windows in the bathroom or laundry room, but they each have lots of recessed lighting and powerful but quiet exhaust fans."

"That is a great idea. It will keep moisture from building up and prevent the possibility of mold." Dale nodded. His face showed approval of the work that Matt had done.

They moved on to see the two bedrooms. One was rather small, but it had a closet and enough room for a crib or bunk beds, a changing table, and a dresser. The other was unexpectedly spacious with a nice walk-in closet. Its large window let in the natural light. They made their way back down the stairs, and then Kristen saw the door under the stairs.

"Is this more storage?" she asked as she turned the doorknob.

"No," Matt began to answer. "It is a—"

"A little bath! How cute!" Kristen squealed.

"It's called a half bath, but maybe this one might be only a third since it is so small." Matt smiled again.

"This is perfect!"

"Well, I thought that a new mom would need to have the basics on each floor. Plus, it provides a toilet for your guests to use without having to go upstairs."

Dale nodded again. "Matt, it looks like you have thought about everything. You really have a gift for designing, and you are equally talented in the execution of your design."

"Well, I learned a lot from your son-in-law. Jason taught me how to look at things and see the possibilities. He has also really encouraged me to expand on my own."

Everyone's comments and smiles belied approval of all that Matt had done.

"When will this be ready?" Kristen asked.

"This one will be ready as soon as we get the washer and dryer in," Matt replied. "So I guess that would be—tomorrow afternoon?"

"Really? Oh, that is great!"

"I would like to have the team see it before anyone moves in," Dale interjected. "I think they would like to see the way these worked out."

"Do you think they could see it before the grand opening?" Kristen queried. "I don't know how long it will be before Maddie's baby is ready to come home, and I'd like for her to be able to move in here before that happened."

Matt's face fell. "I was thinking that this one would be yours. When I was choosing the finishes, I was thinking about what you might like."

"Oh, I do like it. I love it," Kristin said, "but Maddie, she is going to need a place before I do. We have already decided that I would stay with Dad and Mom until my little guy is a few weeks old."

"Then I think I might have the answer. Follow me."

Matt unlocked the apartment next door.

"Behold—unit number two!" Matt swung the door open.

The layout of the second apartment was identical to the first, except that it was a mirror image. The differences were the paint colors, the countertop colors, and the backsplash. The uniqueness of those three items gave this apartment a look all its own.

"It looks like this one is almost done too," Dale remarked.

"It is! In fact, it is done." Matt went on. "It already has its washer and dryer. Mrs. Philers from church stopped me last Sunday and told me that she had just replaced hers with a new front loader. She said that her old pair still worked fine, so I went and got them."

Dale smiled. "Good old Lizzie. She has always had a generous spirit. It's just like her to take an interest in helping the young mothers who will be living here."

"Not only did she donate the laundry pair, but she also gave us some living room furniture and a small dining table with two leaves and four chairs. I had them put into what is, for now, our storage area. I didn't want to impose her style on any of the residents." Matt turned toward Kristen. "Well, do you think this one would work for Maddie and her baby?"

"Oh, yes! I know she will love it!"

"You know, I think I can get the team over to see these apartments in a couple of days. I know they will be thrilled to see what you have done here. And to think you were able to do it with the very conservative budget we gave you." Dale shook his head to show his amazement. "I don't know how you pulled it off."

"Well, it really helped when so much of the building supplies were donated," Matt explained, "and I was able to find some really good bargains at the ReStore."

"Is that the store that Habitat for Humanity runs?" Kristen asked.

Matt nodded. "Uh huh. I took some of the things I removed from my mom's kitchen there, and then I got to looking around to see what I could use here. For instance, those backsplash tiles—they were in a box with a whole bunch of broken ones. I think they must have been dropped from a truck."

"Then they definitely belong here. This will be a place where broken things are made beautiful!"

Dale put his arm around his daughter. "And there is nothing here more beautiful than the woman that you have become."

Kristen hugged her dad, and a tear slipped from her eye. "Thanks, Dad. Right now, with this big boy right here, I don't feel particularly beautiful." She rubbed her tummy, and her baby kicked in response. "Oh, you heard me talking about you, did you?" She laughed.

"I was talking more of your heart," her dad responded. "Now, let's go eat whatever it is that you baked and is smelling so tempting, shall we?"

Just as Matt was locking the apartment doors, Jason and Jodie arrived with the meal in a picnic basket.

"Yes! We are late again," Jodie remarked as she lifted the car seat out of the car. "I assure you that we will get better at this. Tardiness will not become a habit."

"Here," Kristen offered. "Let us take that food and Elsa Hope to the break room while you two tour Matt's handiwork."

They all enjoyed Jodie's meal, and, as usual, Kristen's experiment was a hit. She put the rest of the cake into an airtight container and slipped it into the refrigerator. "The crew can enjoy this tomorrow on their breaks, and I will bake another one that we can start selling at Grounds for Hope.

The team from the church, along with about twenty others, toured

199

the two completed apartments. Matt's craftsmanship was admired by all. The ladies all oohed and ahhed, while the men checked out the cabinetry and finish work. They were impressed by the extra soundproofing that he had done between the backs of the apartments and the church auditorium. They all agreed that Matt had made amazing use of the funds he was given. When they were told of the donations by the Philers family, several of the women huddled together and whispered. When they turned back to the group, one announced, "We have decided that we are going to have a housewarming party for Living Hope. We are going to ask people to donate new and good, usable furniture, small appliances, kitchenware, linens, and such. They would be kept here to let the moms choose the things that they need for their apartments."

"That's a great idea, ladies!" Jon said. "All in favor?"

A huge "aye" came from the group.

Chapter 52

Kristen headed for the coffee shop well before dawn. Since she couldn't see any stars in the early-morning sky, she knew they were in for a gray morning. "That's okay," Kristen said to herself. "It means that our grand opening customers will be ready for some nice hot brews." She was grateful that two of the college team had volunteered on their own to come in at 4:30 a.m. to prep for the big day. Kristen and Jodie had baked scones late Sunday afternoon. Jodie had agreed to make the scones when Kristen would be out of commission. That way, Kristen's recipe would stay in the family. She hoped that they had made enough for today's predicted rush.

As she drove, she thought of Maddie's "Showtime!" on their soft opening day, and it brought a smile to her face. This was her dream—the coffee shop, the apartments, and helping young single mothers. She neared Grounds of Hope and could see that the lights were already on. Every now and then, she would see one of the employees moving quickly with a tray of coffee cakes. "This is my dream. It has come true." She nodded. Then a new thought came to her, and she spoke it out loud. "No, this is not *my* dream—it is God's work." Many people had invested their time, their money, their expertise, and their generosity into this, but it all belonged to God. She sat in her car and silently thanked God for all that He had done to make this possible.

With an audible "It all belongs to God," she got out of the car. She had noticed that each day, it had become a bit harder to get into and out of the driver's seat. She glanced at the back seat where the baby seat had already been installed. "Soon, my little guy will be there with me." She rubbed her hand over her belly.

Kristen called her crew together and told them that she wanted to start their day with prayer. "We're already ahead of you, Kristen," Krystle quipped. "We did that almost an hour ago."

Pleased that this crew of college kids could carry on so well without her, Kristen said, "Well, then, since I didn't get in on that one, would you pray one more time with me included?"

"Just because you weren't here didn't mean you weren't included. We prayed for you too," Joel responded. "But we will pray again with you here."

After a brief prayer, the crew spread out to complete the morning's preparations. In less than an hour, they would be officially opening their doors to the public.

The sun tried its hardest to break through the cloud layer but just couldn't quite make it. The day, however, grew brighter, and the temperature was pleasant. Many of the patrons were pleased to make use of the outdoor seating. At the peak of the crowd, the line inside numbered eight to ten and was about ten deep outside the door. Maddie took the orders and ran the cash register. Randy, it appeared, had a real knack for filling the incoming orders, and along with Susan, efficiently served the customers. His confidence spilled over to Joel. Krystle made it her mission to keep the tables and floor clean. Kristen greeted the customers and decided that she would be the one to take over for breaks. She soon discovered that she herself needed a break. Taking her latte to the conference room, she sat in one chair and propped her feet up on another. "Okay, little dude," she said aloud. "How about letting your momma have some rest." She closed her eyes and sipped the enchanting caramel flavor of her drink.

Maddie came in just before she needed to leave for the hospital. "Are you okay?" she asked.

"I think so. I just did a bit too much this morning. I was trying to be everyone and do everything. I guess it got the best of me, and this little guy is letting me know."

"Maybe you should go home for a few hours," Maddie suggested.

"Agh!" Kristen bolted upright.

"Or maybe you should go with me to the hospital. Are you sure you are not in labor?"

"No, no." Kristen shook her head. "Really, I just overdid it. It was a muscle twitch in my back. I just need to sit here awhile."

"Well, okay, but make sure you rest. The crew is doing just fine, and Krystle is here. You know she can work circles around any two of the rest of us."

Kristen laughed. "You're right about that. I can't believe how busy we continue to be."

"I know. This is all so exciting! Almost as exciting as my being able to move in this weekend. I think maybe Geoffrey will be able to come home at the end of next week. He has really been hitting his benchmarks lately." With that, Maddie left to spend the rest of her day at the hospital.

It was hard to tell when the noon rush started or ended because of the continuous stream of customers through the door. The soups went fast, and several were disappointed that they could not have the one for which they had been waiting. The sandwiches were eagerly eaten. Many commented how they had heard of the great lunch menu from someone who had been there the week before. The huge scone stockpile was depleted by noon, and the coffee cakes were almost gone as well.

Shortly after two, Kristen nearly doubled over as a pain shot through her back. This pain lasted longer—not the brief stab like the last one. "Please, not now. I can't go into labor now." Even though she was full-term, she had been certain that the baby would hold off until after the grand opening. Her midwife had told her that she probably had at least one more week. "First babies," she had said, "typically take their time arriving."

Kristen found it difficult to be of much use for the rest of the afternoon. When the shop closed at three, the crew met to evaluate their first day's experiences. Kristen jotted down notes as each added his or her opinion. Through their efficient teamwork, it took less than thirty minutes for the crew to have everything cleaned and ready for their second day. When everyone had left, Kristen began gathering the things she needed to take home—the dirty aprons and towels, her computer, and her rolling crate. When she experienced two more episodes of back pain, she realized that what she was experiencing was more than just the effects of doing too much that morning. She called her mother at work, and Bonnie wasted no time in coming to pick up her daughter. "I stopped by home and picked up your bag," she said. "From what you told me, I think we should be heading right to the hospital. I think it's time for a baby boy."

"You might be right," Kristen managed to get out before another contraction stopped her short.

Upon arriving at the hospital, an orderly appeared with a wheelchair. Bonnie assisted her daughter into the chair and then went to park the car in the temporary lot for obstetric patients. She was told that she could leave it there until Kristen was checked in and they got an update on her condition. *Her condition?* Bonnie thought. *She's having a baby, for Pete's sake. That's her condition.* She laughed aloud. Inside, she was directed to the birthing center, where she spotted Kristen sitting in front of the admissions desk. By the time Bonnie got there, she was ready to be wheeled down the hall to a room. The lady at the desk said that they would be checking her out in the observation room and then would be deciding if she would be formally admitted. Bonnie nodded and quickly followed the chair to the room. She placed calls to her husband and Jodie. Both were excited about the news but said they would wait for an update before they headed out. Jodie suddenly realized that this meant that she was on scone-baking duty.

The midwife confirmed that Kristen was in labor and that she was far enough along to admit her. The news brought a weak smile from Kristen, but it also brought a sense of fear of the unknown and a realization that she was about to take on another full-time responsibility. What a comfort it was to have her mother there with her. Bonnie smoothed her daughter's hair and asked what she could do for her. Kristen's little baby boy finally made his entrance into the world shortly before 11:00 p.m., with both Bonnie and Jodie there to encourage the new mother. Dale, Jason, and wee Elsa Hope waited in the family area.

It was nice to have a normal delivery of a full-term baby. Jodie had spent so much of the last two months in the NICU, seeing babies who were struggling to live, and then taking home and caring for a preemie, that she had practically forgotten what normal was like. She now looked at her sister with her healthy baby boy and marveled at the ways their lives had changed in the past year.

"Does he have a name yet?" Dale asked as he reached out to hold his grandson.

"Not quite yet." Kristen laughed.

Jodie joined in the laughter. "You know how it takes us Peterson girls a little time to get to know our babies before we decide on a name. Don't you remember that we had some of our dolls for nearly a week before we named them? We had to get to know them first."

"Well, okay, but don't let me go too long calling him Little Buddy." Dale touched his grandson's tiny nose. "We don't want that, do we, Little Buddy!"

The next day, the family gathered again at the hospital. Kristen had asked for them all to dress up a bit. "Do you know what's up?" Jason asked his wife.

"No, but I bet it has something to do with a formal introduction to our new nephew," she replied.

Dale and Bonnie were already fawning over their grandson when the Iglands arrived at the room. Kristen looked totally refreshed, having her hair done up and wearing nice street clothes.

"How did you get away with not wearing the hospital gown?" Jodie asked.

"They are planning to release us as soon as my midwife signs off, but I wanted to do something as a family before we left."

"Enough of the mystery," Dale said. "What is that something?"

"Come with me." Kristen got up and motioned for them to follow. Carrying her baby boy, she led them toward the fountain outside the chapel.

"When Jodie was here, I discovered this spot, a place where the stained glass in the chapel let in light, and the fountain trickled its happy melody." Kristen motioned with her hand. "Here is the perfect place for a family photo—the generations of the Peterson family."

"Oh, I think so too," agreed Bonnie.

"But first," Kristin continued, "I want to introduce you all to Jakob Dale Peterson."